Easiest If I Had A Gun

Easiest If I Had A Gun

Stories

Michael Gerhard Martin

Printed in the United States of America.
10 9 8 7 6 5 4 3 2 1

FIRST EDITION, November 2014

ISBN: 978-0-692-29400-0

Acknowledgement is made to the following publications, in which these
stories originally appeared: *Bayou Magazine #61*, May 2014: "Shit Weasel is
Late for Class"; *The Ocean State Review*, summer 2014: "Seventy Two Pound Fish
Story"; *Junctures:* "Even the Dust"; *Yawp!:* "You Gotta Know When to Hold Them."

Alleyway Books
an imprint of
Braddock Avenue Books
PO Box 502
Braddock PA 15104

Cover photograph: Julia Sapir, www.JuliaSapir.com
Cover design: Karen Antonelli
Title handwriting: Emma Dumont
Book layout: Victoria Venskoske

www.braddockavenuebooks.com

Distributed by Small Press Distribution

For Gerhard Martin, who told me to find work I liked, because I'd have to spend a hell of a lot of time doing it.

Acknowledgements

"Bridgeville," "Dreamland," "Made Just For Ewe!," and "Shit Weasel Is Late For Class" were all written under generous summer stipends from Babson College, and I received another to work on the final drafts of this collection. My chairs, Kathleen Kelly, Mary Pinard, and Elizabeth Goldberg, all worked tirelessly for more just compensation for adjunct professors, and the requirement that I write stories for my dinner has been a welcome caveat. So, I thank the Babson Faculty Research Fund and everyone who made those grants possible. They changed my life.

My in-house developmental editor—and wife, the poet Ellen Goldstein—has read my stuff, praised my efforts, killed my darlings (quickly; they barely felt a thing), submitted stories to journals without my knowing, schmoozed my publisher, endured my sense of humor, and helped me find a safe warm place from which I can write.

I wish to thank my readers, Liz Champlin and Brandy Whitlock, for knowing my work so intimately; and my colleague and friend, Rachel May, for giving me a ton of shit whenever I whined about rejections.

The Johns Hopkins University Center for Talented Youth has been my home for twenty summers. I had my first fiction workshops at their summer camps when I was a child, and I returned after my first year of teaching to mentor prodigies. Nerd Camp is the game I play when I sit down to write, and it is the place I return to when I realize an accomplishment.

Chuck Kinder is a grizzled little old hillbilly, but don't let it fool you—that man is dangerous. If someone can find a way to get this book to whatever mosquito-infested south-Florida swamp shack he's holed up in, I'm sure he'd trade you a couple of pelts for it, like as not kill you, probably. Chuck and Diane, I love you.

Michele Gorman Boyd, I'm sorry I didn't come to the IU trailer the first couple of times you summoned me. You have never steered me wrong.

I dearly wish Bud Stock and Buddy Nordan were alive to see this.

* * *

"The Strange Ways People Are" was a finalist for a *Glimmer Train* Short Story Award for New Writers, and "Made Just For Ewe!" was a finalist for the Nelligan Prize. This collection was a semi-finalist for the Hudson Prize and a finalist for the Iowa Short Fiction Award and John Simmons Short Fiction Award. "Shit Weasel Is Late for Class" won the James Knudsen Prize for Fiction from University of New Orleans and *Bayou Magazine*.

Table of Contents

Shit Weasel Is Late For Class

After fifth period theology, Brian McVey backs me up against a painting of the Virgin Mary and smacks me around while his toady, Billy Moyer, calls color. I think it's because I stopped saying the Pledge of Allegiance. I told Mrs. Henderson, my homeroom teacher, that I wouldn't recite it because I thought it was dumb to promise anything to an inanimate object, that it violated my religious beliefs by being idolatrous, and because I had come to the conclusion that most patriotic displays were nationalism dressed up seductively. She looked tired and said she was fine with me just standing there. I am fifteen, and I have read all of George Orwell's essays.

Billy Moyer says, "Your fat ass is getting kicked, fatass."

McVey says, "Commie pussy," and needles me in the ribs. Most of his punches are just jabs, only little nips of pain and fear, but I hate being a punching bag, especially in front of other kids. I hate his hands on me, pinching, flicking, poking. I hate his locker-room smell of sweat covered over with Right Guard. I hate being one of the weird ones, hate being the kind of kid who gets bullied by Burnout Brian McVey.

I muster some venom and say, "You two will be the first against the wall when the revolution comes," and they look confused. Brian retorts by flicking my ear and knocking my glasses off, and then they move away, jostling smaller kids and kicking a backpack down the hall before them.

I get to English as the bell rings, and slide into the seat next to Kate Lavelle, my new workshop partner. I am falling more in love with her with every essay draft. She can draw. She can write. She acts in plays at other schools, she plays the viola, she

1

loves Elvis Costello. I can smell her honeysuckle shampoo; she has lank chestnut hair and enormous brown eyes, and she also has some junk in the trunk and a weak chin, so I think I have a chance.

Before McVey turned mean, it had been a kid named Jayme Lake. Before him, a kid named John Quigg bounced a basketball off of my face and waled on me at Boy Scouts. I had taken a turtle that he wanted to smash with a rock and flung it into the woods. But besides the physical stuff—the hard pinching of my nipples, the flicking of my nuts, the slaps and trips and pushes, the outright punches—there is an undercurrent buzz, the message, like synchronous pulses from a thousand little transmitters, that I am a loser. I am a virgin. I am fat, a freak, a geek, a tard, a brain. I am the kind of kid who absolutely must not let any girl know he likes her, because she will have to make a retching noise and say "Gross!," and never speak to him again. I'm infectious, and I know it—if she likes me, if she goes out with me, then she'll be a target. They'll write that she is a tranny on the bathroom wall, give her a humiliating nickname, put disgusting things in her hair and on her chair and in her bag.

I've been wanting to ask Kate out since Christmas. I sit there feeling bruised, wanting to cry and glad that I don't. When it is time to mark up drafts of each other's essays on The Great Gatsby, I compliment her on her transitions and her diction. She writes, "Josh, I never would have thought to compare King Arthur and Gatsby! Sooooooo cool!" She has drawn a caricature of me on a horse, carrying a lance tipped with a banner that says "Super Genius." I don't even try, though, and I hate myself for it all day. I make up a story, that I am nobly sparing her the torment and humiliation, but it's hollow. I'm lonely. I want to date a girl—this girl, who likes me for some reason. But I feel like shit. I feel like I am shit. I wish that I were dead, mangled beyond recognition in a school bus accident, maybe, or popped like a balloon by an oncoming train. I think about being run over by a combine harvester, and it cheers me up a little. How do you get a thousand dead babies into a refrigerator?

The next morning, in second-period social studies, I take careful notes with my stainless-steel art deco fountain pen. I got

2

into this program at Dickinson College in the summer, and I did pretty well, and my mom bought the pen, to encourage me, I guess. It has a weight and balance that I love, and I am getting better at letting the nib float on a cushion of ink just above the page.

Mr. Welder wheels out the rickety metal TV cart and shows us a grainy home-made tape of Ronald Reagan telling Gorbachev to "tear down this wall," and he keeps stopping it every fifteen seconds to tell us about the Red Menace, so I raise my hand, and when he calls on me, I say, "I was reading the Communist Manifesto, and, like, doesn't Karl Marx sound a lot like Jesus? Like the gospels, the beatitudes, I mean. You know, when Jesus talks about the poor? Isn't Communism, like, more Christian than Capitalism?" He gets agitated trying to explain my error, all throbbing temples and red cheeks and wagging mustache. I like him—he is one of my favorite teachers—but I am bored, and messing with adults is a hobby. After class he asks me to stay, and searches his bookshelves until he finds a copy of a book titled One Day in the Life of Ivan Denisovich. He looks at me with genuine concern and tells me he wants me to read it, and then come back to him and tell him what I think. I read the back cover and nod, thinking I know exactly what I will tell him—that it is a thinly veiled bourgeois-reactionary attempt to undermine the glorious people's revolution. I can't help myself.

In homeroom, which is also the biology lab, we sit in orange theater seats on risers, so that the back of my head is level with the knees of the kids behind me. I feel the pen slide out of my pants pocket. I turn to look for it and get slapped upside the head. Then my Parker lands in my lap with the clip twisted halfway off of the cap. The delicate nib is smashed, ruined. All of this happens while Mrs. Henderson is reading announcements; she doesn't see a thing.

Billy Moyer hisses, "Why do you have to have a special pen, fatass? Why can't you just write with a regular pen, you fat fuck?"

During the announcements, Brian McVey hits me again; and then again, each time Mrs. Henderson glances away from our side of the room. Sometimes slaps at my ears, sometimes hard punches to my head. If I try to leave the classroom before he is gone I will get punched in the stomach and kidneys, and I worry about being late for class again. I think that I shouldn't be punished because Burnout Brian is a dickhead. I think what a loser I'll be if I tell, but I am already a stupid fucking loser. So I decide to go to the dean, Mr. Allito. I wait in his office until he comes in, saying, "Mr. Geringer, what can I do for you?"

I look up at the kindly man who is quick to anger, and I say. "Someone bent my pen."

He looks at the pen and says, "That's a shame. Did you try to bend it back?"

"No," I say.

"Well, is that all?"

My mouth is dry and I feel the urge to turn and run. I want to tell him something, but I can't form the words. He sends me to class with a signed late slip.

As I'm turning to leave, he says, "Mr. Geringer?"

I turn and look at him, "Yessir?"

He leans on the counter separating us and looks through his thick glasses with his bushy eyebrows furrowed. "Josh, I don't know how to say this, but you don't really seem to—to try to fit in." He pulls in a breath and holds it. "Maybe things would be easier for you if you, you know, didn't always try to make it a point to be so," he searches for a word. "Just, ah, go with the flow, you know? Just try to fit in. Don't make waves all the time."

I know he means well, but what he doesn't know is that I have been trying all year. I have been talking less in class, I've let my grades slip, and I have lobbied my parents hard for contact lenses. I have been eating spoonfuls of things my mom's magazines say burn fat, like horseradish and apple cider vinegar. I don't read in public anymore. I have been starving myself and taking ex-lax. I cut my shaggy hair and went for a clean-cut part, but I didn't get the Harrison Ford look I was after because I have a doughy round face and tons of acne. I have been trying to keep my mouth shut. It just isn't in me. While he is speaking I imagine marking up his pep talk like an essay, with phrases like "avoid clichés" and "is this really the argument you intend to make?"

Leaving the dean's office, I almost run into a wall of huge Polish farm boys from St. Mary's. One of them says, "Hey! Josh!" and I get a little freaked out, but I nod and smile at Mark Ossosky. These kids are tractor trailers, monster trucks, bulldozers. But they don't pick on kids. Mark, especially, is smart. He is squat, with a square head and really, really bad skin, and he doesn't get hassled. He has muscles like a horse from slinging hay bales. He is going to prom with Katie Altenderfer, and they are a couple now, and I wonder if they are in love. She's smoking hot.

I say, "Hey, Mark," and he says, "Wait, wait a minute! Hey, you guys, this is the kid—Josh—he got the highest SATs." I resist the urge to shush him; everybody knows, but I still think I can live it down.

One of the other boys, taller and just as thick around in the arms and chest, says, "High five! Mark got the highest, whatchacallit, TSWE." His voice booms in the tiled corridor.

My hand stings with his approval. "I heard, yeah, awesome. Congratulations, man. Congratulations." He beams at me. I know they don't mean any harm but I am afraid of them anyway. I feel myself flushing red, so I paste on a smile and retreat to class.

At home, off the bus, I let myself into the house and go straight to my room. I take off my uniform trousers and my blue acrylic school sweater, my Oxford shirt and my Mickey Mouse tie. I take off two layers of too-small t-shirts that I have pulled from the donation bags my mom always forgets to take to St. Vincent DePaul. I stand in front of my mirror in my underwear, trying to find something that isn't bad about myself. Something that isn't weird or gross or ugly. I think that if I had a sharp enough knife, maybe I could give myself liposuction with my dad's Shop Vac—how much different could it be? It would hurt, sure. I'd have to go to the hospital, but they wouldn't put the fat back in. I decide to skip dinner. I get on the floor and do a dozen clumsy sit-ups before I am winded. I bite my hand as hard as I can to stop from crying, and I muffle my face so my sisters won't hear and tell on me. My mom has threatened to take me to a shrink if I keep crying.

I come in the next morning, and my books and notebooks are gone from my locker. I panic, and a passing frosh says the same thing happened to Dan, the kid who wants to be a physics professor, and to James, the kid with the Joan Crawford obsession. This frosh tells me that McVey was bragging about standing behind us and watching us open our lockers to get the combinations. The frosh says, "That kid is a fucking dick."

I go to Mr. Allito. This time I tell him that it was Brian, that he's been picking on me and the other boys, and that he's taken our books. He makes me sit in the foyer to his office while he calls McVey in and slams the door. I hear him yelling for a long time. Brian comes out, Mr. Allito hovering over him like a red-faced bird of prey. Brian tells me where my books are hidden in the library, and mumbles "I'm sorry."

Seeing him upset and scared, seeing him in trouble, feels good. I beam, shake his hand, say "Apology accepted." Mr. Allito asks us to pray with him, and we fold our hands and bow our heads as he says an Act of Contrition, which I think is mainly for Brian, because what the hell did I do? I am just glad that it is finally over. And it was so easy.

It takes an hour and a half for Brian to corner me. This time it is a knee to the balls, my head banged against the wall of the corridor, sharp toe kicks to my thighs and ass. I am gasping and crying—he hits me again and again, always hard jabs at the soft parts.

He grabs at my chest, pinches hard, and says "You have titties like a little bitch." He hisses, "What are you going to do, Gay-Ranger? What are you going to do, pussy? Tell on me?"

We change cycles for third period, and I finish my typing class with an S+. Now I have six weeks of gym to look forward to, and when I get to the bleachers, Brian is there, pointing me out to his cro-mag friends. I think that it would be so much better to kill myself than to go through the doors of the locker room. I try to keep my head down, but he comes up behind me and gropes my chest, yelling, "Who wants to play with the faggot's titties," while I squirm and try to break out of his embrace. I try to be fast. I do not shower; I wear my shorts and t-shirt under my school clothes. By Wednesday, they have broken into my locker to smear what looks like Elmer's glue on the crotch of my dark blue uniform pants, and I have to cut chemistry to wash them in the sink and dry them with the hand dryer. Ten demerits and an automatic detention. I have never had a demerit before.

The first Friday of my gym rotation, Brian and three other

guys surround me, poke me, grope me. Brian yells, "Who else smells Gay-ranger? Gay-ranger doesn't take a shower because he's afraid of showing us his titties!" I don't even know half of their names, but they push and jostle me towards the shower. They pull my shirts off, my tight layers, and slap at my boy-tits, pinch my nipples. They force me onto my back on a bench, and a kid with a unibrow sits on my chest and my stomach and bounces up and down. Then Brian tells them to hold me. He drops his shorts and spreads his ass cheeks and sits on my face, rubbing his asshole on me, dangling his scrotum in my face. He turns around, exuberant, and I try not to cry, really try, but the tears won't stop.

"How do you like that, faggot?" he says, and he high-fives Unibrow, who is laughing so hard he can't stand up straight. I grab at my clothes on the floor, getting dressed as best I can. I'm blind with tears and their voices are like the roar of water over rocks. I get out into the hall. The bell rings. I go to the boy's bathroom and scrub at my face with the gritty pink soap that smells like bleach. I wash out my mouth and my nose, I gag, I puke a little into the sink. The soap burns my eyes. When I have put myself together I go and get a late pass, and Mr. Allito tells me that I have another detention, that I had better clean up my act.

Monday, I still have to go to gym, I still have to sit in front of him in homeroom. He goes for me constantly, flicking ears, whispering "faggot" so girls can hear, punching me hard. I stand up, turn. He smiles and says, "Come on, homo." I turn around and sit down. I don't know how to fight, and he is strong and fast and meaner than I am. I am a complete piece of shit. A pussy. I deserve the sharp raps to the back of my head. I wish I were The Karate Kid.

On the way out of homeroom he rabbit-punches me in the kidney, and I spin around and shove him so hard he falls backwards into a shelf of lab glass. For a moment I imagine him cut and bleeding, and I like the idea. He recovers his balance lightening fast, and hits me three times in the face, harder than I have ever been hit by anyone. He is going to work me over some more but Billy hisses, "Dean!" They are gone before

7

Mr. Allito turns the corner. Our homeroom teacher has no idea what happened. I have a bloody nose, but I get bloody noses a lot. I rush to the bathroom, where I cry and spit out blood from a cut cheek and clean my face with wet paper towels. I rinse with cold water and hope I don't have a black eye. I don't ever want to come back to this place. I don't want to be me. I want to kill myself. I have been thinking about it a lot lately. I think killing myself would be easiest if I had a gun. I think of one I know, at the bottom of a drawer that smells like oil and cedar. I think I could just put it to my temple, pull the trigger, boom. No more of this heinous shit. When I come out in the hall, my bookbag is leaning against a locker.

My grandparents take me to Zern's on Saturday night. Zern's was once a regional market center, but now it's a flea market—produce stands amid stalls selling antiques, biker clothing, used cameras, bongs, underwear, socks, coverless books and magazines. They'll sell porno to anyone. It smells like too-ripe fruit, pipe tobacco, leather, sweat, roasted nuts, and smoked meat. Huge sausages curl like boa constrictors. I tell my Nana that I am going to the comic book store, and she tuts and draws on a Salem Light and says, "Don't waste your money on that shit." I find the guy who sells ninja throwing stars and machetes. I think about how cool it would be to chop off Brian's head with a sword, but it just isn't practical, and swords are expensive. I spend eight dollars on a flat metal paratrooper's knife. In my room, I sharpen it with a whetstone I learned to use in Webelos. I think about using it to cut myself, tracing the point over the blue lines in my wrist. I practice sliding it open with one hand, stabbing at the air, at an imaginary Brian McVey.

In homeroom on Monday, I bear what I think might be the last humiliation. I try to think about McVey in fantasy-novel terms—I think of him as a foul Warg of Morgoth, think about slicing him open, ending his villainy with a twist of the blade and bright white light, cutting treasure from his ruined carcass. Magic. But I don't do anything with the knife. I am afraid to start this, because I don't know how to fight with a knife, not really. In homeroom he claps my ear, and I hear a dizzy ringing. I'm nauseous. I am a coward.

These huge Polish kids, Mark Ossosky and Dave Duda, corner me after lunch.

Ossosky says, "We hear you've been having some trouble with McVey." I mumble something and try to duck away, but Duda has arms like albatross wings and he blocks my way. I cringe, but he is smiling at me, saying "It's okay, buddy, it's okay."

I feel my face turn hot and red. I don't want to cry in front of these guys. I squeak, "I don't want to talk about it!" and hate the sound of my voice.

They are not mean—Duda calls me "buddy"—but they keep me there and make me tell. I won't tell about the locker room, though, and no one can make me. I guard that shame like treasure.

I carry the knife to homeroom again. I think that if I do it, even if I just hurt him, that will be okay. Maybe I'll go to a special school—who cares? People are asking people to prom, and I almost ask Kate, but one of her friends has already fixed her up with a kid from the Hill School, and I think I don't deserve to go with her. She'll be a joke and a target. Me going to prom is another joke. I'm a joke.

My grandfather has a pistol he bought when he was a civil defense coordinator after the war, forgotten under some sweaters in his dresser. I get Nan and Pop to drive me to the Atlantic Book Warehouse in Montgomeryville, where I score a remaindered copy of The Gun Owner's Bible for four dollars. I slip it in with some ex-library copies of Frank Herbert novels and a dog-eared Bloom County collection.

I think that it would be hard to do it with a knife, but that a gun is just like a remote control. I steal the pistol while Nana is cutting hair in the shop at the back of her house and my grandfather is dozing in front of the Phillies game in the living room. I identify it as a Colt 1911A1, a .45 caliber automatic. It is heavy and solid and smells like machine oil. I learn to eject the clip, to check the chamber, to flip the safety catch on and off. I cock it and wrap my hands around the diamond-textured wooden grip. My hands fit. It feels natural; I am old enough, big enough, that this grown-up weapon fits my hands. I catch a ride to Kmart with my Nana, and while she is buying sheets and looking at the back-row clearance piles, I pick up a Winchester White Box of hollow-tip .45 slugs. No one notices, when I plunk down the last of my Christmas money on the sporting goods counter, that my hands are sweating and my pulse is hammering in my ears. At home I oil the gun, clean it, learn to snap bullets against the stiff spring to load the magazine, snap the magazine into the grip feeling like Dirty Harry. I quick-draw at the figure in my mirror. I point the loaded gun at my head and hold it there, my eyes closed, my index finger resting on a slim crescent of blue steel, my breath like cold wind. I open my eyes. I hold it at a downward angle, line up the sites and do my best Clint Eastwood: "What do you think, Brian? Do you feel lucky?"

I have the loaded pistol in my bag at homeroom. I have not fired it—too risky—and I feel a sick thrill of anticipation. I am ready to do it or to not do it. I will reach into my bag, rack the slide to chamber a round, turn, and pull the trigger. I want to do it. I tell myself, today is the day you are going to destroy Brian McVey. I don't just want to hurt him, I want to destroy him. I want to be safe. I want to blow his brains out. I want his brains splattered on the wall.

But McVey isn't there. Billy calls me a fat-assed faggot, but he doesn't touch me. I'm happier than I have been in months. The pistol is a flat weight at the bottom of my school bag. In a bathroom stall, I drop the clip out and pull the slide back to make sure the chamber is clear. I nearly forget that it is there for the rest of the day.

I bring it to school the next day, less sure, wondering if I just show it to Brian, if I make him afraid, maybe he will leave me alone. I think, again, about killing myself, which seems much easier. But if I am not angry, I am sick and trembling, and I would rather be angry. I want to make him afraid and then to hurt him, to destroy him, to blow his brains out. I really want to.

In homeroom, Brian's face is bruised and his arm is in a cast. He won't look at me. He doesn't talk to me. I begin to understand. Later, I find out that some kids took him into the wrestling room and broke his arm on purpose, figuring you can't pick on nerdy kids if your arm is broken, if you know that worse things can happen to you, if you have been told to lay off in a way you aren't going to forget. Burnout fucking losers don't get to pick on smart kids. I feel like singing in the hallways, throwing my books in the air and dancing. In English, I ask Kate what she is doing for the weekend, all sly and matter-of-fact, but she is going to Connecticut to visit her grandmother, so I bide my time. She brushes against me, warm and soft, when she goes into her bag for her vocab book.

A few days later, Billy flicks my ear. He is slower than Brian, and I am sitting two feet lower in the orange theater seats, so when he does it again, I grab his finger, then his wrist, and pull him over my shoulder. He falls into the row of giggle girls in front of us, all spindly limbs and girls pushing him away like he might give them leprosy. He gets demerits for being disruptive. McVey leans way over to thump me in the head with his cast, but he can't do it very hard, and when I turn to look at him, he looks like he is in pain. I whisper, "Your mother sucks cocks in hell," and move my tongue against my cheek. His mother died when he was a little kid, and he hates his stepmother, so now he is really pissed. There is a rumor that he is close to having enough demerits to get suspended, and this close to the end of the year, that means summer school in every class. I think that I am more than willing to test that hypothesis. I can get eighty more demerits, no problem. He kicks at my chair, but it doesn't bother me. He kicks at my head and I grab his leg and hold it and say "Ow!" long enough for Mrs. Henderson to see him pulling his leg back from the kick. I can feel a scrape on my face, and I hope it shows. A kid in the next row hands my glasses back to me. Perfect.

Mrs. Henderson says, "Brian, what the hell are you doing?" She tells him to come to the front of the room, and he makes his way out of his row with a lot of clumsy shuffling, trying to balance with his busted arm. I hiss, "summer school," just loud enough to set the girls in the second row to hear. Brian is red, red, red, and there is nothing he can do. I can barely sit still, barely keep from standing up and pointing, giving him the finger. He's off to see Mr. Allito. He's fucked.

In the hallway, red-faced Billy tries to punch me in the gut, but scrapes his knuckle on my belt buckle and shakes his hand. He's not a tough kid, and I have thirty pounds on him, easy. He says, "I guess you think you're some kind of badass because you got someone else to fight your fights, you fat fuck."

I pick him up by his shirt front, feeling strong for the first time ever, feeling giddy, and I shake him, smack him off of a wall, and push him down half a flight of crowded steps. The gun is back in my grandfather's dresser. Billy struggles against a sea of people. The bullets are hidden in the attic of the garage. I see his face for a moment, and he looks like he is drowning.

I start smacking Billy around like it's my varsity sport. I bring in a water pistol and soak the front of his trousers, and when he turns and clenches his legs together, I get him low on the seat of his pants. I feel bad, for moments, here and there, but I am learning how many people were afraid of Burnout Brian, and how many people hate Billy Moyer's guts.

I sneak up behind him and pull his books out of his hands. Other kids start doing it too, and still others kick them down the hallway. I start chanting his initials, "Beeeeeee, Emmmm," and he becomes BM Billy. I push him down in the hallway and say, "Butt Boy Brian can't help you, BM Billy," and the kid with the Joan Crawford fixation laughs his best Snagglepuss laugh. Later I hear this senior girl start calling out "Weeeeeeeeasel," and I am delighted when I learn that she means him. In hours he is Wheezy, then Wheezy BM, and in a few days, just Shit Weasel.

Shit Weasel is late for class. Shit weasel gets demerits for not taking care of his textbooks, and his parents have to pay for the worst one, a chemistry book I kick into a urinal. I don't always feel good about what I am doing. And then, when I start to feel low about it, I think, "You know why I know how that feels, fuckhead?" Kate is dating the guy her friend set her up with, and she is drawing portraits of him in her notebooks.

I use a marker to draw a cartoon of BM Billy sucking Brian's cock on the wall of a stall in the boy's room, and we have an assembly over it. By the end of our talking to by Monseigneur Close, every kid in the auditorium knows about it, knows it was Billy in the picture. Every kid in school is imitating Monseigneur Close saying "depicting an immoral act" over and over. People start calling it out to Billy. He becomes Immoral Act, BJ Billy.

Dave Lourdes, a feather-weight wrestler, starts saying hi to me in the hallways, shadow-boxing me and calling out "Josh-ooh-ahh," which I take to be friendly. We sneak up on BJ Billy while he is talking to Faith O'Connell, grab his pockets, and haul down on his pants. We're just trying to get them down over his hips, but I pull hard enough to rip the back pocket right off and the front of his pants open, Billy flailing at my head and whining "Guys! Seriously! Stop it, guys!" Dave whoops his high-pitched laugh and Faith can't help herself, she titters with her hand over her mouth as Billy tries to hold his pants together and limp down the hall to the boy's room. He gets detention for being late and demerits for ruining his uniform trousers. I am sure he is going to tell, sure I will have to hang my head and pretend to be ashamed. The truth is, I do feel a little ashamed, but I hate Shit Weasel more.

Billy gets a long lecture about cleaning up his act. He doesn't tell.

He comes up to me in the grey-tiled hallway, just two weeks of classes and another of finals left, and he apologizes. He actually puts his hand over his heart and says he is sorry, and he asks if we can put everything behind us. He tells me he knows how he treated me was wrong. Billy says, "Please."

I say, "Sure, Billy," offer him my right hand, and when he takes it I pull him towards me and trip him. His books fan out across the tile floor, and I give him a sharp little toe-kick in the hip, pinching his skin against the bone.

I say, "Wheezy, you of all people should know, that isn't how it works."

The Strange Ways People Are

My dad is one of those dying people who has begun to live life backwards. He gets hospice, so you know he's a goner in less than six months. He got $10,000 in a lawsuit from the Union. That's a little over a thousand bucks for every round of chemo.

It started out funny. Louise, his second wife, kicked him out of his retirement home—"the double-wide," my son says—and Ernie and I took him in. That's not funny. Her kids tried to get him to sign over his power-of-attorney and his doctor made up a reason for him to stay in the hospital for a few days until we could get a room ready. He was still with it then. It was horrible, really.

What was funny was when he called her "Kitty," which was my mom's name. She sat there in all of her makeup, with her hair blued and her sweatshirt with the rhinestone flowers glued to it, looking more like Ethel Merman than my scrawny little ma, and said, "No, Duff, I'm Louise!" over and over again. He just smiled and looked at her as if he hadn't seen the woman in front of him for years. Louise started up about putting him in a home again after that, and then she stopped visiting altogether. Dean, my brother, went to her trailer and carted off Dad's mower.

Jake's my other brother, the handful. With Dean you just lock up the valuables and listen to him babble about his satellite dish and his new grandson.

Dad's been peeing in a bag for a while, and he's got to wear a Depends now, and you have to be nice and sit and talk him into having his movements. He wants to sit on the bowl. He says, "Where are my pants, Gott dammit all!"

Jake stands there like a basketball coach in his salesman clothes, with his beet-red face. He says, "Just shit in the sheets! Just shit in the sheets!"

Dad says, "No gottdammit, where are my pants?" Except for his thick Dutchy accent, he sounds just like my Ernie some mornings before work. This goes on for a while until I get Jake to shut up and I lean down and say "They're in the dryer, Pop-pop. They won't be ready for a while," and he gets quiet and doesn't ask for them again. I tell him to relax, do his business, and then he lies still and sleepy while I change him.

Before he goes to sleep he says, "I wish I had my gun." He looks deflated, loose skin melting across bone.

I say, "Please don't start that again, Daddy." I'm thinking he means suicide. He's not scared of the priest anymore. He's had his last rites a few times before, and in his mind, what's left of it, God can't keep his part of that bargain soon enough.

He says, "I'd shoot that Jake, Gott dammit all. Aiy-yai yai."

When we're alone sometimes, I'm my mother and we are on vacation. At first it was hard because I miss her too, in spite of everything. Then it was easy, because I feel like a mother again taking care of him. It's strange. That isn't lost on me. There is beauty in the strange ways people are, I'm convinced of it.

Dad says, "Kitty, what are you doing? You'd better pack— we're leaving for Connecticut at five for Chrise-sakes." I was just a baby when they went there, but I think of the trip I took years later; something about New England made me feel wonderfully unlike myself, and I have to wonder if it didn't have the same effect on Dad. Later the central air is on and the whole place stinks because I am steaming clams. He says, "Gott dammit, I am going to eat them clams I caught!," and I don't see the point in arguing because clams are cheap enough at the IGA. Anything to get him to eat.

Jake drops in, sees the brown butter and says, "Why don't you just feed him a Happy Meal? Why not just give him a cake of lard and a spoon?" Jake wants to call an ambulance for every little thing. He calls the hospital raving like mad, and the doctors won't talk to him.

I'm in pain too. And this isn't the first time I've felt like

15

shooting Jake myself.

Ernie pulls me close in the dark. He smells of machines and sweat, my father long ago minus the sweet smell of manure that farm girls either come to love or despise. Sometimes he reminds me of everything I escaped the farm for. Tonight I will him to be a comfort, I lie still and stiff with fear that he will not. His feet, still in their black socks, find mine. He says, "Go to sleep, Elsie."

"I can't," I say.

"What should I say?"

"Nothing. Nothing." A fear so terrible it is blasphemy. There isn't an answer.

The curtains are drawn against the glare. His eyes are sensitive. Dad says, "Kitty, the boy needs to learn." I slip into character. Sometimes I'm Rebecca of Sunnybrook Farms. Sometimes I'm Anne of Green Gables. Sometimes I want a weak tremolo like Kate Hepburn in *On Golden Pond*, like Mom before she died.

I say, "Learn what, Duff?"

He gets angry. "Don't play dumb," he says. "He's got to learn. But I didn't mean to hurt him." I think I know what he's talking about, and I try to think of something to say to divert him. Instead I say, "You shouldn't have, Duff."

He starts to cry, real tears and a face like a scream, sharp breaths and sobbing. I should be unnerved. Dad despised crying; instead, I feel as if I am watching something forbidden and fascinating, like the punching of a cow to relieve colic or the slippery birth of still lambs.

Jake's oldest boy joined the navy after Jake hit him in the head with a shovel for wasting the gas in the push mower, and now we hear he's down there with the Mexicans, some kind of holy-roller missionary. I know what Dad's talking about and I can't bring myself to put my arms around him. There is this part of me that finds his suffering easy to see sometimes. He deserves a lot of it. Jake and Dean couldn't see this; Dean is a fool and Jake is a monster. If either one of them stopped to think it would kill them. I've already started to think. I need to think more than I ever have. It is a skill a person can, for her own reasons, try to lose.

I hated being a farm girl, the kids of car salesman and dentists from Pottstown staring at my father as he walked the halls of my high school on the soles of high rubber boots. I am not stupid, as my mother and father thought, not a heifer to birth and milk babies and help with the canning and cooking. But who'd know it?

There are so many things I want to know myself, before my own children take advantage of my senility to put together my mysteries.

He says, "Kitty, those grubs are going to kill the weeping cherry."

I say, "Don't worry about it now, Duff." I can't believe how much I sound like her.

"I need a can of chimney pitch," he says. "I need it Kitty. Please Kitty. That tree, Kitty, that tree is my pride and joy. I spent years on that tree." Of course I know what tree he's talking about. I can imagine the farm where I grew up without any difficulty, from the gooseberries and the chicken coops to the marsh below the house, and the woodshed. I can imagine the weeping cherry, the veil of blossoms and the exotic twisting of the branches and roots. When I was a girl, just looking at those roots was like curling my toes in black soil.

"The boys already did it, Duff. Everything's fine. The tree is fine."

He cries softly. "Those goddamned grubs," he says. "They don't care how hard you work. They don't care for nothing."

In the Catechism I had to memorize, they go on and on about The Mystery of the Trinity, that God can be Father, Son, and Spirit and one being at the same time. I used to go up in the orchard and lay on a flat rock and think of things like that, God, the opening of blossoms, the decay of fallen fruit. I dreamed that heaven was a library, rows and rows of answers to childish questions and all the time in the world to ask them. This is the only mystery that I know: sometimes a good and beautiful person will act like a mad dog, and sometimes a mad dog will act like a good and beautiful person.

He says, "Kitty, if I pick gooseberries, will you put them up this week?"

"Next week, Duff," I say. "Let them go another week for jelly."

He smiles and seems to rock in his bed, though it may just be my imagination. He was always a rocker.

He says, "Kitty, you're the most beautiful woman in the world. Did I tell you that today?"

I say, "God, no, I'm not." Ma wasn't, and neither am I. Ma had thick glasses and thin, ragged hair all of her life. She was thin and pale and shook like cattails in a breeze. I was scrawny and homely in my homemade clothes, with my big flat rear end. Now I'm getting old.

"You always say that, but it ain't how I see it."

On my way home from work, while the hospice nurse sits with him, I take a detour. I live about three miles from the farm where I grew up; so, now that I think of it, does my dad. Kids pull up behind me fast, and before I think I put on the brakes. They honk and swerve to pass me under the close rows of old trees. I can't breathe, and then I remember I can. I listen for a skipped beat and wait to see if there will be a pain on my left side. I can remember when this was dirt, then gravel.

The new owners have let the yards and gardens in the front go. While Mom was dying all of those years, dad kept the yards looking like pictures from a magazine. Parked across the road, I can almost see his small figure at the top of the hill, and as he comes closer he seems not just to grow larger, but older. At the top of the hill he is a young man moving quickly, his shotgun slung over his shoulder. As he approaches the piles of junk the new owners have deposited on the lawn, he bends under some weight. He stops to look at that weeping cherry; he always stopped to look at it. By the time he reaches the front walk I, the youngest, am already grown and married, and Mom is small and frail and almost gone to her diabetes and MS and all of those terrible infections. An old man already dying of cancer, he reaches the door of an empty house. This is the memory I choose, my poor dying father. I could as easily picture him dragging Jake or Dean up that path, imagine being tied upside-down from the rafters of the barn by my brothers, every one of my mom's biting words. Things I've said to my own kids, and things they've said to me. I could as easily loathe them all.

I am sitting with my dad when Ernie comes home from work. He comes in and kisses me, then turns to Dad. Ernie leans on the steel railings of the bed. We keep them raised so that he won't fall, in case he forgets he can't move. Dad's eyes focus through puddles of Visine. He says, "Ernie."

Ernie says, "Yes, Duff?"

It takes my dad a few moments. Then he says, "We been friends a long time, vut?"

"Aye-yes, we have. A long time." There are tears in my Ernie's voice.

Dad comes alive. He rattles the rails of the hospital bed. He says, "Then let me out of this goddamned cage."

"Kitty," he says, gruff.

I have a business making teddy bears and dolls for some gift shops out in Lancaster. My son talks about my sweat shop, because I've got so many orders that my mother-in-law sews the little dresses. I'm sitting, embroidering, counting dollars with stitches and estimating for my next supply run to Walmart and Michael's Crafts. It is a moment before I reply.

"Kitty!" he seems to scream, though there isn't a true scream left in him.

"Yes, Duff," I say.

"Why in hell does a girl want to go to college?" he says. "Tell me that, gott dammit." I stop midstitch, and the little flowers I'm sewing on a white dress—like a christening dress, I suppose— look suddenly obscene. He is red and moving his arms and legs. I think for a moment that he will work himself in to a heart attack, and that will be the end. He's got a living will.

Then, when my head clears, when I've played out (for how many times?) that scene, "*You'll be a secretary at Flaggs until you get married, gott dammit, and if you want to say another word about it you can go sleep in the barn.*" I say, "She's got the brains, Duff." I feel the tips of my ears burning. I think of all of the shit I've cleaned up in the last month, all of the urine I've poured off, the nights I haven't slept.

"What's the use of it?" he says.

"She wants to go," I say.

"What doesn't a child want?" he says. "This isn't what you said before. Who's filling your head with this crap?"

Then I am up and yelling at my Dad. I don't care if he is dying. Right now I feel as if I could kill him myself. "Noone is filling my head with anything! It's an education, not a toy, god-dammit."

He looks at me placidly for a long time, and I think for a moment he's worked himself catatonic. Then he takes my hand softly. "All right," he says, "All right. She can go. We'll send her." I clap my hands together and feel a great weight escape my heart. He says, "She's probably the best of the whole goddamned bunch of 'em." Then I realize that I am forty-six years old and playing dress-up for a senile old man who can afford to make promises like a politician.

"Elsie," he says. "Elsie-E-I-E-I-O!"

I am startled. He's been calling me Kitty for weeks. He's been calling everyone by different names. I say, "Yes, Dad?"

He says, "Elsie, I'm dying. I really am."

I say, "Yes, Daddy, you are," very softly.

"I'm not in any pain, really," he says.

"That's good, Dad."

"No way for an old man to live," he says. "Gonna die like a dog, an old hound dog." He stops for a minute, and I think he may have drifted off. I wonder if he's just died. He breathes and I get up to wipe a little Vicks under his nose. "Jezzus God, do you remember how that one, vutsisname?, stank up the porch when he went under there to die." He smiles his bloodless smile, sweet and far away. "Gott damned dog, *ach du leiber.*"

"Oh, Dad," I say. What else am I going to say?

"Ashes to ashes, dust to dust, if the Lord don't get ya, the devil must." He laughs until he coughs, then stares until he sleeps. I sit next to him and go back to stitching smaller dreams.

Made Just For Ewe!

Elsa waited at the door with a full rolling cart of stock that smelled like Spanish moss and dried eucalyptus, reading a self-help book for small business owners. A Mexican girl in a security uniform, her sleek curls pulled close at the nape of her neck, was pacing slowly in front of the big steel doors, looking bored. Elsa looked up and joined the other merchants in giving her the eye. The book suggested that she think of a word that defined the mission of her business, a single word for what she was trying to bring to the world—just one word that she could repeat to herself for inspiration.

She thought, "Failure," and her jaw tightened. She had lost $6000 on a rained-out craft show the week before, and their home equity line of credit was maxed. She was operating at a loss. She was operating, she thought, on blind faith; faith that the doors would open, faith that the people would come, faith that she would be able to retire some day. Faith that she would keep her home. Faith that she would die before she ran out of money.

"Why can't they let us in a few minutes early? What could it possibly hurt?" she wondered to the woman behind her.

"God forbid!" the woman said. Elsa searched for her name, and remembered it was Cynthia. She sold tacky glitter snowman sweatshirts. Cynthia pitched her voice at the security guard and said, "For six thousand dollars, God forbid they let us set up fifteen minutes early!" A murmur ran through the crowd. The Mexican girl was pretending she hadn't heard them, but Elsa could tell she had.

She glared at the girl and thought, that's what I'm paying for—to have somebody keep me from setting up, to have somebody keep me from making money. She looked behind her at the lengthening line, and saw her husband's red shirt bobbing towards her in the distance. She needed glasses, but she knew it was him by his walk, which reminded her of a sandpiper she had once seen at the Jersey shore. She flapped her arm until he gestured with the Styrofoam coffee cup in his left hand. He was balancing a box of Krispy Kreme donuts in the other—they had discovered Krispy Kreme while scouting the show three years before, and the chain had not yet come as far north as Pennsylvania. He handed her the coffee cup, three creams and two sugars, and she washed down her blood pressure pills.

At seven-thirty, a huge black security guard came out and gave the uniformed girl a nod. She opened the doors and Elsa helped Ernie push the cart over the threshold.

Ernie had been allowed in the night before to assemble the canopy. The display racks and shelves stood like the mangled skeleton of some huge animal. She wheeled her flat-bed cart around behind the stall and unloaded the color-coded Rubbermaid totes that held her setup supplies. Ernie went out to bring in a load of merchandise.

She worked methodically, stopping for sips of milky coffee and bites of fried dough, standing on a plastic step-stool, pinning and tacking fabric and ribbon and ultra-realistic-looking faux pine garland to every surface and support. She hung her crackle-painted sign above the entryway: "Elsa's Little Extras (Made Just For Ewe!)" with a dignified sheep depicted between the lines of text.

She finished decorating the stall by eight and told Ernie she was going back to the trailer for some boxes. She wheeled out past dozens of couples putting their displays together, listened to the soft clanking industry of cottage crafters starting one of the big shows. The security guard held the door and smiled at Elsa, and Elsa smiled back, thinking about how even though they were so different, the Mexican girl was probably a Catholic, too—and so pretty if Elsa looked past the long fingernails and the greasy kiss curls pasted to the girl's cheeks. Slender. Elsa imagined her in a muslin peasant dress, all brown cheeks and glittering eyes, gazing up thankfully at some handsome cowboy hero. The same girl was there when Elsa came back with a cart loaded with boxes, and Elsa beamed at her as she heaved the cart over the aluminum threshold.

By eight-fifteen she was ravenous, and the stall had taken on a thatch of dried flowers, lace, and calico. She arranged angels, made from antique wooden industrial yarn spools, on a high shelf. She hung punched-tin lanterns beneath the eaves. The spool angels were hers, original, and she or her mother-in-law sewed every dress. The lanterns had been candleholders until Ernie wired them up. They cast a pretty mottled light around the inside of the booth, but Elsa wondered if it would be too dark for the older ladies. She grabbed a clamp lamp and attached it to one of the canopy supports, ran the cord to a power strip, and adjusted it so that it wasn't too conspicuous.

While Ernie got out the credit card machine, Elsa hob-knobbed. She was excited to see the candy man, Saul, set up across the aisle from her. He had both tea tree gum and anise bears, candies she missed from when she was a girl. And he always bought spool angels, every single time she saw him. She didn't really like licorice, but loved the lighter taste of anise bears.

She couldn't remember the name of the Candle Lady when she poked her head into the shop, but Elsa recognized her smell: gardenia mixed with sugar cookies and pumpkin spice. The Candle Lady admired one of Elsa's faux-pine centerpieces, fingering the real pine cones and velvet ribbon. "Tug on the needles," Elsa told her. "Go ahead . . . see, no needles on your tablecloth. Add a candle with a very light pine scent, maybe some eucalyptus and wintergreen—all natural, of course." The woman asked to have one put aside, and then added two matching wreaths and a garland, three angel dolls, and a bedside lamp made from an electric candle and an oversized Ball Mason jar. The candle had a silicon-dipped bulb that looked, in the words of the wholesale catalogue, "like a real flame seen through an antique float-glass window." The two women traded cards, and the Candle Lady said she would have some scent samples for Elsa later in the week, that she would be happy to sell her an exclusive scented line, that she would even take some of the centerpieces to resell at other shows.

Saul came over and asked her if she had any spool angels done in blue for Chanukah. She pointed to one on the shelf that had a blue brocade vest and a star of David in place of the round halos of the Christian angels. "I have a bunch more in the car; Ernie can go get them."

"Can you get me six, Elsie?" he asked. He was a plain man, older, bald, but Elsa liked his beaky nose and broad grin. "My wife and daughter want them for presents."

She said she would, and wrote it on the list for Ernie when he finally arrived: "Ten Jewish angels." She figured Saul would probably change his mind and take at least a couple more. She'd had the idea for the Jewish angels at a show in New Jersey, where the familiar Santas and snowmen on old women's jewelry and sweaters gave way to six-pointed stars and menorahs. The Jewish stuff sold like hotcakes because no one else had anything like it. That was her little something extra; that was why she had been a success. When everybody else started to show up with knockoffs of her best sellers, she'd have boxes of something new to roll out ready in the trailer.

Ernie came in at ten to nine, and she had $735 worth of merchandise stacked and labeled for other merchants. That was just under eighteen percent of her stall fee, provided all of them came back; she hoped to gross between twenty five thousand and thirty, and needed ten to cover her costs.

She decided to scope out the show and do a little shopping. Ernie had his laptop open and hooked it to the credit card machine. She told him she was going for a walk, and he looked up and said, "Get me something."

Thirty yards down the aisle, she admired a beautifully embroidered hand-knit woolen pullover at a stall where a slim blond woman was clipping metal arms into a garment display.

Elsa said, "I like this very much. The yellow stitching at the middle of the violets is a nice touch. Will you hold it for me until after the opening bell?"

The woman looked at her, then back at the rack. "Are we allowed to do that?"

"Just as long as we don't exchange money. That's what the Saul, the candy man, told me."

The woman said she would, and Elsa shook her hand and gave her a business card with her stall number inked on the back. She also wrote "15% off for my fellow merchants, all week long!"

"Do you do the embroidery yourself?" Elsa asked.

The woman nodded, and Elsa could see she was younger than she looked at first. "Me and my mom and grandma. We kept coming to these shows, and it was all the same stuff, so we decided to give it a try. The whole place is so full of cheap foreign junk," she trailed off.

"Tell me about it!" Elsa said. "We have to wait for the stroke of nine to sell to each other, but if some of this crap is handmade, then I'm Chinese."

"I know! I'm like, yeah, you have a plastic Santa factory in your garage, right?"

Elsa laughed. "I'm Sherry," the blond woman said. "I" sounded like "Ah" to Elsa's ear. She introduced herself, and Sherry said, "It's nice to meet you. People up here aren't friendly at all."

Elsa asked the girl where she was from, and Sherry told her that she and her mother had driven up from northern Georgia the day before.

Elsa had not been popular as a girl; she hadn't been pretty, or good at anything that other girls didn't make fun of. In school, they would flip the back of her collar to prove to one another that her clothes were homemade. Eating home made cupcakes, she had coveted their Tastykakes and Twinkies products.

Here, people knew her. She spoke their language. They admired her taste, her work. She made friends.

She got another coffee and some Krimpets at the concession stand. It was run by the promoter so it could open early to serve the merchants. The coffee was thin and sour, but the promoters were the only ones allowed to sell anything hot, so that's what there was. Tomasso Entertainment Enterprises raked off for space, raked off for concessions that competed with the merchants who sold food, and raised their rates every single year, even when business was terrible. She was waited on by a black girl who Elsa decided was probably about seventeen years old, and the girl didn't seem to even see Elsa as she plopped down the Styrofoam cups and packages of butterscotch and peanut butter cakes. Elsa didn't put anything in the tip jar.

When she got back to the booth Ernie handed her the keys to the little safe he had wheeled in behind her register table. She started every show with $300 in coins and singles, because the local banks wouldn't make change for merchants unless they opened accounts.

She settled in for the rush.

By ten after nine, the tide of women lapped against the pilings of Elsa's shop. She noted that they were overwhelmingly older women and their adult daughters. Predictably, the credit card machine was slow, and Ernie was busy taking manual imprints that they would enter into the little computer later. And the cash mounted up—twenties were piling up in the safe, which always made her nervous. She took checks, which was a toss-up: they cost her nothing to deposit, unlike the credit card transactions where the bank raked off three or four percent, but inevitably some trash would pass her a bad check and never make good on it.

Faith.

It slowed down around lunchtime, and Ernie took the cart back to the trailer to restock the booth. He brought it back four times, waiting on customers while she re-hung display items and organized the register supplies. As it settled down, Ernie went out to pick up some Chinese food, and after they ate, they packaged their cash in ATM deposit envelopes. They banked with a large company that had offices and ATMs in several states. He also took the credit card slips to a Starbucks where he could get reliable internet to enter them. They had covered their fees in the first two hours, and they kissed before he drove off with the battered black nylon bag that held the notebook computer. Elsa's pulse was racing.

She went to the front of her shop, took a twenty out of her cash apron, and stood behind some customers at Saul's Ol' Tyme Candyman booth, her hopes set on dark chocolate fudge and anise bears. The woman in front of her wore heavy make-up over a powder-white complexion, and was maybe 40 years old—younger than Elsa by over a decade; she reminded Elsa unpleasantly of her mother-in-law. Saul got to the woman, a broad smile across his lean face, and said, "What can I get you dear?"

"Nigger babies!" she said. Her voice was nasal, and she pronounced her words as if her mouth were already full. "Two pounds! I haven't seen nigger babies since I was a little girl!"

Elsa jerked her head around, terrified some brown person would hear the word and go berserk. She felt short of breath, a tightening in her chest that reminded her of church, of the dark confinement of the confessional booth. She hated racial slurs with the same intense heat and shame with which she hated dirty words for procreation and words for people's privates.

"Oh my god, nigger babies!" She watched the woman preening like Queen for a Day, and Elsa gasped and fumed. The woman got her bag of candy. The purple-black gumdrop bears glittered with clear crystal sugar, and Elsa thought the woman looked obscene as she sucked down two at a time.

Saul rolled his eyes at Elsa and said, "What can I get you, Elsie?" She didn't let anyone call her Elsie, but she forced a smile at him because she liked him. He was dignified; he was a gentleman, Mr. Bingley in a yarmulke. "Hi Saul," she said as loudly as she could. "I would like a pound of anise bears, please." She turned a glare on the woman, who was wandering away, shoving candies into her mouth.

Saul snickered and bagged the candy. "Sad thing, they really did used to call them that, some places," he said. "It's like this guy in Western Pennsylvania one time, he asks me if he can 'Jew me down' on twenty pounds of candy for the little league, and he's totally serious – has no idea, none whatsoever." Saul snickered again, wagging his head. Elsa could imagine chagrin with the intensity and vivid detail of a childhood trauma; she thought it was because she had gone to Catholic school. She gritted her teeth, hunched her shoulders, and imagined slapping the blond woman's dirty mouth.

"Elsie, you hear the one about the professional crafter who won big in the lottery?" She shook her head no. "She vowed to keep setting up at shows until the money ran out."

She chuckled in spite of herself. "Business okay for you?" she asked him.

"Yeah, you know, not what it was four or five years ago, same as everybody."

"Yeah, tell me about it. I sold a ton of American flag merchandise after 9/11, and I had all of that fireman stuff that went like hotcakes, but now I can't give my stuff away at some of the shows."

He bagged her candy, handed it across and said, "Well, ya know, what comes around."

She smiled and noted that Saul put his candy in paper bags. It was a very nice touch. It made the bulk candy, much of it sold by the same distributors as a more or less popular item for more than a hundred years, into a piece of yesteryear. Nostalgia, Elsa repeated silently. Nostalgia, Nostalgia, Nostalgia. That would be her word. Nostalgia would describe her enterprise, what she hoped to bring into the world, what it would do for people.

Back in her stall, she looked at one of the purplish gumdrops covered in crystals of sugar before she slurped the first bear down, thinking that it didn't look like anything, really. Not really a bear, and certainly not—she found herself about to think "nigger," and she shut her eyes and tried to clear her head.

A few minutes later a woman entered, shoving the last of a hotdog into her mouth and pointing at the shelf of angels with her free hand. "I want the green one, the blue one, and the yellow one. And that wreath," she mumbled, pointing. Elsa gathered the items, packed the wreath in a box expertly, wrapped the spool angels in bubble wrap—could she get heavy brown paper, or maybe butcher's paper, or should she stick with bubble wrap for its superior breakage protection? —and took the woman's card. Her expensive cellular credit card machine worked for once, spitting out a receipt for the woman and a confirmation code for Elsa's records. She smiled at the woman, who was already gathering more items—rusty tin stars in different sizes (where to get the big twenty-eight inch ones was a trade secret Elsa guarded jealously), gourds hand-painted like snowmen and Santas, and a pair of old leather ice skates sprouting dried bittersweet vine and green velvet ribbon. Elsa punched numbers into her register, tore off the receipt, and ran the card again for $128.54. The woman squinted and brought her face very close to the paper to sign her name, and Elsa stamped a little sheep onto her receipt. She helped the hotdog woman load her purchases onto a low rectangular cart like the one Elsa used for restocking, and the woman said "Merry Christmas" and walked away. Elsa saw that she had cleverly used bungee cords to make a sort of cargo net between the front and back handles, and noted the way the cords were spaced and interlaced.

The hotdog woman was good luck. Elsa racked up sale after sale, most of them multiple items, many of them over $100, reaching a crescendo with one sale for over $400 (half of that came from the sale of footstools cleverly hidden inside antique-looking stuffed sheep; her design, Ernie made the wooden forms, and she sewed the sheep, which were supposed to look like black-faced Suffolk ewes. Chinese imitations would appear at Walmart in October of the following year).

The afternoon brought a steady downpour of customers, and Elsa struggled to restock the displays and check people out. She got more and more upset with Ernie for abandoning her, and the anise bears were making her sick. She needed to go to the bathroom, and she felt an unpleasant thrum in her temples. And then she saw a woman stuffing small items into a canvas shopping bag. She was orange with fake tan, her nails were manicured, and she wore high heel boots. First Christmas ornaments, then little sleighs with runners cut to look like reindeer, and then she was working on a Santa gourd, trying to figure out how to put it in the bag.

Elsa puffed herself and shouted, "May I help you?" at the shoplifter. The woman got the gourd to rest inside the bag and scanned the displays as if for her next purchase. She reached for a tiny handmade birdhouse with a realistic looking bird (they were Malayan, made with real feathers), and began to slip it into her bag. Elsa grabbed the handles and pulled the bag off of the woman's arm. "Thief!" Elsa shouted. "Thief! Security!"

The woman pulled harder on the bag, and said, "Fuck off! Give it!" She pulled with all of her weight, and Elsa held on until the bag handles came loose, spilling Elsa's merchandise under the feet of the two women. The shoplifter turned and ran through the crowd, and Elsa glared after her as bystanders picked up the trampled decorations. She felt her face flush, and gulped for breath. An old woman put her hands on Elsa's shoulder and gently said, "There, now, it isn't so bad," and Elsa realized the woman thought she was sobbing, so she did. The painted gourd was badly scratched and several less expensive items were crushed.

Ten minutes later an enormous black man dressed like a park

ranger was talking to Saul, who pointed him to Elsa. He ducked his head under the canopy of the stall and introduced himself in a drawl: "Hello ma'am, I'm Sergeant Watkins, head of the security detail here. I'd like to ask you some questions, if that's alright with you. Did y'all have a shoplifter?"

Elsa looked up at his eyes, his shiny-dark complexion, his wall of marine corps muscles, and nodded. He said, "She get away with anything?" Elsa shook her head; she was still short of breath. He held out a Polaroid of the woman she had tussled with, and said, "That her?" In the photo, the woman was shoving stuffed animals into the pockets of her long coat. Elsa shook her head up and down vigorously. "She break anything?"

Elsa peeped "yes," and showed him the pile of damaged merchandise on her table. She gave him the bag, which contained a few pieces of someone else's tacky junk, and her broken merchandise. He wrote down her name, her stall number, her business address, and her phone number. He asked, "Did she assault you in any way? She lay hands on you or anything?"

Elsa shook her head, no. She said, "What will happen now?"

"Well, local cops come in and scare her. If she signs a confession, we let her go to stand a court date, and ban her from all Tomasso Entertainment events. This one got no warrants, so we don't get to see her go to jail. Up to me," he said, "I'd put them all away for a hundred years."

Elsa suddenly found her voice. "What about my money? Are they going to make her pay for the things that were damaged?"

"We will do what we can to recover your merchandise," Sergeant Watkins recited, "but Tomasso Entertainment is not responsible in any way for loss due to fire, theft, or any other damages."

Elsa knit her eyebrows. "Oh well then. I'm out money and you just take down her name and let her go?"

"And ban her for life from any and all Tomasso Entertainment events. She comes back, she gets prosecuted for criminal trespass, no joking around. I can try to get the local policeman to write up damages in the complaint, but good luck getting paid. She'll get fined and sent to some kind of program on a Saturday morning."

Elsa felt cold anger, shrugged and mumbled "I have things to do." She left Sergeant Watkins standing in the front of her stall. She had a line, and she worked steadily, trying not to lose business just because she was old and slow. Ernie wandered up, shoveling popcorn into his mouth. He said, "Hiya. How's business?"

She hissed, "What does it look like? Wait on some people, will you?" She felt herself flushing, and she tried to control her breath. She slid one set of packages over the makeshift counter and started totaling the next customer's purchases, expertly protecting each piece. Ernie fumed next to her—she had meant to make him angry, and she noted his anger with satisfaction. He called, "I can help who's next," a little too loudly. He used up too many of the bigger boxes, wrapped things in too much bubble wrap, and sent people away with a mess of tape and cardboard that made her hate him. She pushed past him to get another roll of bubble wrap from behind the displays and he said, "Ow, watch it god dammit!"

She hissed, "Shut up for Christ's sakes."

He said, "Well then don't push me over, for cryin' out loud!"

She glared at him, pushed past him again, and together they whittled away at the line until it became a trickle. Then Ernie stayed at the till while Elsa frantically hung new stock on her displays and worked through her adrenaline and blind anger. It had been a good day. Ernie was stuffing cash into the drop safe as they heard a scream from the booth next door.

People in the aisle outside the stalls stopped and craned their necks, but Elsa couldn't see what the commotion was all about. She saw half a dozen security guards push through the crowd. People who couldn't see past the crowd eventually gave up, and her shop was packed with impatient customers. Saul and his workers were hustling, too, filling bags with nostalgia and raking in cash. After half an hour she heard shouting, and the crowd broke up as two men in Thurmont Police Department windbreakers ordered them to move on, and then entered the neighboring stall.

The customers thinned out after four thirty, as the Senior Center charters loaded back onto their buses and headed to the nearest Morrison's Cafeteria or Old Country Buffet. A middle-aged black woman was looking at the angels perched on the shelf, and a woman Elsa presumed was her mother wandered up to join her. Elsa thought how there were a lot more black people at the shows down South. She was used to seeing Mexicans and Asians and Indians at shows in Pennsylvania and New Jersey, but never so many black people. The older of the two women pointed at the pinkish-white wooden ball that served as the head of one of the spool angels, looked at Elsa, and said, "Don't you have any that are flesh colored?" She laughed a dry little cackle, and the tips of Elsa's ears burned red. The paint tube was, in fact, labeled "Flesh Tone." Unbidden, she imagined a tube of paint labeled "Nigger," and hated the woman from Saul's stand, hated her father's expression, "I worked like three darkies today," hated her brothers' jokes, hated the men in white hoods who marched in Boyertown and Pennsburg every couple of years. She stretched a smile across her face and tried to talk, but no words came out of her mouth.

The younger woman said, "Don't mind her," and smiled warmly at Elsa. "I would like a few of these with, uh, brown faces. Do you do them that way?"

"I do," Elsa lied. "But not here. I mean, I don't have any left. I can see if my husband can find some more. Are you looking for any particular colors?" Elsa flashed warm, felt her ears get hot. "The dresses, I mean. Any color you want them in?"

"Burgundy would be nice," the daughter said. "I like that dark green velvety-looking one, and I like the blue."

"They'll take whatever colors we get for them," the older woman said brightly, and she cackled again. Elsa smiled for real at the sound, felt like the woman's laughter could sweep her up. She had to pee.

Elsa left Ernie in charge of the stand and went walking, first to the bathroom, then to the van. She drove to an A.C. Moore they had passed on the drive in, and bought brown, white, and yellow paint in plastic bottles, and artist's brushes, and a few plastic bags full of other supplies. Black—no, African American—angels! Her mind raced. Asian angels? Why not—a few anyway. She'd paint little lines instead of dots for eyes, and give them black straight horsehair wigs—she wondered if ying-yang halos would be too much, and decided to try a few and see how they came out. She wondered how to paint Mexican faces, wondered what elements she could introduce to appeal to them. She looked at some packages of little sombreros and decided they were tacky; if she were going to do it, she'd do it with more class.

She stopped at the drug store to buy some Tylenol and a fingernail clipper, dawdling, paying Ernie back for disappearing on her. She joined a line of customers waiting at the only open register, and glared at the cashier who was talking loudly into the phone. She was a tall white girl in her early twenties, broad-shouldered and pale-skinned, wearing the kind of goggle-like tinted eyeglasses she knew were popular with young black women and with MC Hammer on Hollywood Squares. The girl's huge breasts lay atop her distended stomach as she stretched and told the caller, "He say he don't want no Steve or Davey. He say he want his baby have a big strong nigga name like Tyrone." She barked a laugh at the phone and started to ring the old woman at the front of the line. The customers in the line shifted uneasily, except one black man. He was younger than Elsa, with just a little grey at his temples, wearing a very fine silk and wool houndstooth jacket and brown wool dress pants. He turned around and looked for someone to laugh with; he was biting his lower lip, and he slapped his thigh and let out a high, almost girlish guffaw. Elsa tried not to meet his eyes. She flushed red, and looked at her shoes. She looked at his back, how his shoulders rolled with stifled laughter under that exquisite fabric, and marveled at his reaction. As quietly as she could, she made her way to the back of the store and paid for her purchases at the pharmacy register. She was breathing hard, and stopped in the stationary section to calm down.

In the trailer that night, parked in the fairgrounds lot with the vans and trailers of the other merchants, Elsa mixed various shades of tan and brown, and Ernie painted six dozen wooden balls. She rejected the first black one he painted because the eyes looked garish and spooky and the pert red mouth obscene. She dug through the bag of yarn she used to make the hair, and experimented with a black wool with a shiny finish until she was satisfied that it looked as good as the blond and red-haired angels they would join on her displays. When they were ready, she replaced the heads of white angels with the brown ones. The wings and clothing were the hard parts; the heads and faces were pretty much interchangeable.

They watched reruns of Law and Order and JAG (which annoyed Elsa because JAG was the same damned show but in a military setting) and then went to sleep early. Elsa had a dream that she was a small child in a crib, and a rat was gnawing at the wicker, trying to get in. She flailed in her sleep, panicked, and Ernie woke with a start and knocked her off of the bed and onto the floor. They both held their breath, suddenly alert in the close cool darkness, the quiet whir of the propane heat pump the only sound. Ernie turned on the dim, yellowish lights and Elsa stood up. Finally, they lay back, and while Elsa did not think she had slept, she woke with the alarm at seven-thirty, to the smells of Spanish moss and eucalyptus and stale husband. Her hip was fitted to Ernie's paunch, pushing her own to the side in a way that made her think of the discomfort of pregnancy. She'd been thin as a rail before the kids.

At least it was warmer in Maryland. New England in the twenty-four-foot cargo-camper had been too hard on her. In Maryland her feet were okay, and her hands weren't too cold to work.

Dozing, waking, she thought about those poor girls who worked for Triangle Shirtwaist. Putting her feet into her slippers, she decided she'd watch the DVD on her portable player once things died down for the evening. She liked the sepia photographs, the frozen laughter of stern faces in documentaries about poor girls who became part of history; and she liked knowing that they had no idea that they would be remembered, that they would meet such a romantic end.

The shower-closet in the packed camper was better than it looked, and she was fresh and wearing clean clothes in less than half an hour. She checked her watch, put some mousse in her short brown hair, smoothed foundation over her acne scars, and brushed her teeth again in the tiny little sink. She took a can of Diet Coke from the mini fridge, and made sure her pill minder was in her purse.

She poked Ernie awake and said, "You have to get going. I need you showered and on the floor by nine-thirty. Make sure you shave."

He heaved himself up and words leaked from him like a tire deflating: "Whatd'ya want to eat?"

"Cinnamon bun from Dunkin Donuts. But don't take too long. I'm going to need you. Don't get lost." She kissed his forehead automatically as he sat and yawned.

She pulled a sweatshirt over her turtleneck, went to open the door of the trailer and found it stuck. She pushed and pulled on the handle, but it wouldn't open. She shook Ernie awake and said, "Get up, will you. I can't open the door."

"What the hell do you mean you can't open the door," he growled.

"What the hell do you think I mean?" she growled back.

He sighed heavily and swung his legs around to rest on the floor. They maneuvered past one another and he tried the latch, gently at first. Then he jiggled it more and more forcefully. Finally he held the latch open as far as it would go and threw his soft shoulder against the metal door. After several tries they could see daylight around the frame, and Elsa began to feel hot and claustrophobic. They were trapped.

Ernie worked at it for a few more minutes until the door, now too mangled to re-close, popped open and nearly spilled him onto the pavement. The morning sun was already bright. They stood listening to the sounds of other merchants waking, and noticed tiny cubes of broken safety glass glinting everywhere. Someone had taken a knife or a razor and cut away the heavy black rubber seal that held the window glass in place on the van. Ernie, wearing a baggy pair of army surplus shorts, black socks, and a white t-shirt stretched tight across his belly, ran up and craned his neck. "Jesus Christ!" he whimpered. "My laptop! That belongs to work!"

On the verge of tears, they inspected the door he had just forced, and found deep gouges in the aluminum around the damaged lock and latch mechanism. Elsa sobbed, less with fear and more with an appreciation of how much it would cost—the laptop, the damage, how she knew she would feel sleeping in that trailer again. Ernie held her and said, "They didn't get in. They got the laptop, but they didn't get in." He was upset, and she felt his soft body tighten with rage.

"Calm down," she said automatically. "At least we're safe."

Other couples wandered up and talked about what they had lost: a camera, a television, a laptop, a box of petty cash. Sherry, the woman with the hand-embroidered pullovers, wept openly; they had stolen her safe, which contained all of her cash as well as the slips she needed to enter to claim her credit card payments. "They aren't even worth anything to anybody but me," she kept telling people, scratching at her hands, hunching her shoulders, looking at the ground as she spoke.

They moved all of Elsa's stock inside before the gate opened, taped a plastic trash bag over the broken window, and Ernie went back to hook the trailer up, bungee the door closed, and tow it to a local dealer recommended by their insurance company.

Elsa worked hard all morning, as the charter buses rolled in and disgorged old women and their middle-aged daughters, fat husbands in plaid shirts, brown women in diaphanous shawls and heavy cotton dresses the colors of autumn leaves. Other merchants stopped by during the lulls, and people she'd seen at a dozen shows but never spoken with introduced themselves and offered their condolences, digging for information, asking the same questions Elsa asked herself—Are you afraid? What all did they get? Did you see them? Were they, you know…?

The darker-complected angels sold like hotcakes, and Elsa's worry and sense of loss lessened as the morning wore on. She bought the fudge she'd forgotten the day before, and Saul told her how sorry he was about the robbery. The husband of another vendor brought her a coffee from the concession stand. The woman who had lost her safe stood a fierce guard over Elsa's stall while she went to the bathroom.

While Elsa wondered if Ernie remembered that she needed to be relieved for lunch, three Asian men came into the stall. They were dressed in suits and ties and cheap plastic dress shoes, and when she asked them how they were doing, they didn't acknowledge her. They gestured at her merchandise as they spoke in a nasal language, and the man who wore his hair in a buzz cut kept lifting items—a birdhouse, a spool angel, a painted gourd—up so they were close to his chest, turning them this way and that as he scrunched his neck to look down. Elsa saw what

36

she thought was a brooch pin—maybe they wore brooch pins wherever he was from – but then she saw the little lens imbedded in it.

"Son of a bitch!" she yelled. "Is that a camera? Is that a goddamned camera?" The other men just looked at her as she grabbed his lapel and pulled his jacket open. A cable had been fed through a hole in the lining of his jacket, and a square black box was strapped under his arm. She felt her temples throb with outrage.

"Thieves!" she yelled at them, clutching her chest. "These are my things! My ideas! Thieves!" People glared after the men as they quickly walked away.

Sergeant Watkins ran over with a uniformed Thurmont Police officer in tow. "You have another one, ma'am?" he puffed.

"Just," she said, short of breath from the excitement, "just some damned wholesalers trying to steal my ideas, my intellectual property. But I guess you can't take down their names and ban them from the shows. I guess all the criminals get to go free."

He paused for a moment, and then leaned in and said, "This is Officer Ludley from the Thurmont Police, ma'am. He wants to ask you about the parking lot break-in."

She politely answered Officer Ludley's questions as best she could. No, she hadn't seen anything. No, they had been running the heat pump, and so hadn't heard much. Yes, they'd lost valuables. He wrote down her name and address and cell phone numbers, and gave her the number of the police report so she could give it to her insurance company. He looked at her kindly and said, "It's probably some illegals." It took her a second to figure out what he meant. Sergeant Watkins added, "Mex-cans responsible for a lot of the crime in town here."

She excused herself as the women from the day before returned to collect their angels. They saw the ones on the shelf and cooed their approval. The older one said, "You do have a talent, dear," and Elsa beamed despite her rough morning. She excused herself, and retrieved the tote full of brown angels from behind the stall.

"I'm just crazy about them," the younger woman said, turning a yellow-frocked angel in her hand.

"You know what I'd like?" the older woman asked. "I'd like a whole crèche of these. I don't suppose you do anything like that." Elsa was excited. She had over a dozen totes full of the spools at home, and she knew where she could get little wooden mangers. Nativity scenes would cost nothing to make, and she could sell them for over $200 each. Best of all, people who didn't want to buy the whole crèche would buy angels as a sort of consolation.

She said, "I bet I could. I'll give you my card, and if you want, I can call you when I have a picture to send you. It would be—I mean, it would be seven or eight people figures, some angels, and I could do some realistic stuffed animal-type figures...."

The older woman said, "I'll just make her pay for it." She jerked her thumb at her daughter and cackled again.

The younger woman took a card from her wallet and handed it to Elsa. "Adelle Leonard," she read aloud.

"I'm Elsa," she said, holding out her hand, first to Adelle's mother, then to Adelle. As they shook hands, Elsa noticed that Adelle had acne scars just like her, and that she had smoothed brown foundation over her face to hide them.

Behind Adelle and her mother, a pinch-faced old white woman and her daughter were looking at Elsa's wares. Elsa noted how like a carbon copy of each other the two couples were, and she missed her own mother, thinking about visiting church bazaars with her while she was still alive. It dawned on Elsa that the younger white woman was the fat-mouthed one who had ordered "nigger babies" from Saul's stand just as the pinch-faced woman's gaze lighted on the shelf of angels and she said, "Pick-a-ninnies! Wasn't I just telling you I was disappointed nobody had any pick-a-ninnies anymore?" She turned to Elsa, shouting past the two black women. "I got to have some of those pick-a-ninny angels!"

Elsa felt a hot pain in her throat and a burning in her eyes. The old black woman did not cackle. Elsa felt her gaze pulled to the fierce eyes of the younger black woman, but they could not look at one another. Elsa ignored the pinch-faced woman, smiled as warmly as she could, and said, "I'll be in touch, Adelle. Is there anything else I can do for you?" Her armpits were wet with sweat and her mouth was dry, metallic.

"Hey, how many of the pick-a-ninnies you got?" the fat-mouthed woman said, still trying to push past the black women without seeming to see them. "My ma's got pick-a-ninnies all over her house," she chirped. "I had a gollywog doll when I was a girl I just loved to pieces."

Elsa snarled, "They're not pick-a-ninnies! They're angels!" She looked at the two fuming black women, wondering if they would snap and start a fight, wanting them to snap and start a fight. She would be on their side.

"Look, honey," the pinch-faced woman said. "She has beaner angels! And chinks!"

"The chinks are cute, but I just love the pick-a-ninnies. You could get the chink one for Marcy as a joke. I wonder if she can make me a gollywog doll like I used to have." The fat-mouthed woman turned towards Elsa, cradling the angels, her face lit with the pleasure of memory.

Elsa felt like a moth caught in a huge fist. Her breath was short and she thought her eyes were bugging out of their sockets. She slapped at the fat-mouthed woman, sending the angel dolls flying. And then she was drowning, saw her vision turn red and then darken.

She woke at the center of a small crowd with Sergeant Watkins' powerful hand touching her neck. There was something across her mouth and a hissing sound, and she realized she must be wearing an oxygen mask. Sergeant Watkins said, "You just take it easy, ma'am, I'm a trained first responder. You just lay back and they be here before you know it. You got the blood pressure?" Saul smiled at her encouragingly from behind the brim of the sergeant's hat.

She nodded.

"Thought so. I got the blood pressure too. We goin' to send you to the hospital to be checked out. They gone to look for your husband right away. Candyman Saul is gonna watch your stuffthat okay?" She nodded a little. "You just relax, we gonna take good care of you." She concentrated on breathing, worrying about what the hospital was going to cost, worrying about the sales she was losing as she lay there, worrying about the home equity line of credit, and trying to ignore the formless terror she still felt holding Sergeant Watkins' hand.

You Gotta Know When To Hold Them

Mrs. Loman was the nurse, and she did medical experiments on kids in the basement of the school for extra money. She put a box of combs on one of the extra desks and squeezed her big fat ass in another desk sideways, and combed through each kid's hair without saying why. She separated Kenny and me from the other kids and made us walk up to the nurse's office. Nobody ever wanted to hang around with Kenny. He had more stains on his shirts than I did, and his uniform pants always had holes in the knees. His mom cut his hair, but didn't bother to get it even or anything. One time a bunch of guys caught him jerking off in the boys room and gave him a whirly. I didn't even look at him on the way up to the nurse's office. I didn't want a loser like Kenny to think we had anything in common. I had enough problems.

The nurse called our moms. Kenny's mom came first, even though they lived a lot farther from school than we did. She was wearing one of his dad's shirts from the refinery and smelled a little like gasoline. She tried not to look at anybody, just ran in the office, signed the paper to take Kenny home early, and ran out.

My mom showed up a long time later wearing a new flowered dress with a white lace collar, and pantyhose and blue shoes. She had her hair done up and earrings on. She walked very straight and shook Mrs. Loman's hand. She asked what the trouble was, and I heard it: head lice. Ma said, "There must be some mistake. Where would my son pick up head lice?" Her perfume filled the little infirmary with the stink of rotting flowers. She wore a ton of it because she was paranoid about smelling like gas.

40

Mrs. Loman said they were going around. My mother said, "I think you're mistaken." She pushed my head down on the table and scratched at my scalp. "Look. I don't see any lice."

Mrs. Loman said, "I'm afraid so. Lots of children get headlice." I could see she was trying to be kind, but she wasn't used to it. When she said "lots," it sounded sarcastic, and I got a little red. Ma tightened her grip on my hair for a minute, and let go just before I would have cried out.

"Heathcliff could not possibly have head lice." She had that mad sound in her voice, like when I repeated one of my dad's jokes in public. That's my name. Heathcliff.

Mrs. Loman got out a magnifying glass and showed Ma the little bugs crawling around on my head. That did it. Ma signed the paper and cried all the way home in the car.

I probably caught the head lice climbing around in one of the cars. That, or playing with my friend Andy's pet raccoon. Who knows? I wasn't the cleanest kid in the world, a fact that broke my sweet ma's heart.

She'd say, "How could any child of mine be so utterly filthy? How could any child of mine be such a slob?" I was a great source of embarrassment to her. I once showed up to one of her high-society tea parties covered in motor oil and bee stings.

I couldn't stay out of the cars. Behind our house was the old Erie Lackawanna freight depot, and on the side of the house was where Nick Fleisch kept the parts cars for his body shop. Nick left them open so I could climb in and play Dukes of Hazard. Dukes was my favorite game.

I liked the VW best for driving, because the windows rolled down and it was low enough that I could get in and out without opening the door. But by the time I was twelve, I liked the big rusty Bonneville better than any of the others. I'd watch Dukes on Friday night, and spend all Saturday lying on the back seat looking out of the filmy back window at the sky and thinking about Daisy. Then afterwards, I'd think about her dowry: the boy who married Daisy Duke would become, de facto, a Duke boy.

There could be no better wife. With her sweet caresses came old uncle Jessie's words of wisdom, words that could make any

41

boy a man. With her came Bo and Luke, the best friends you could imagine, and the chance to meet Kenny Rogers some day, if he happened to be on tour and his driver happened to be speeding through Hazard County. With her came moonshine and pig roasts. And most of all, with her came the extra set of keys to the General Lee. Once Daisy dropped the extra set of keys to the General down her bra so that Enis, the deputy, couldn't get them. He was too shy. I pitied her, but I pitied Enis more, for being a dumbass. I'd lay in the back of the Bonneville and try to come up with a way to get an invitation to get inside of Daisy Duke's shirt.

Sometimes I'd get trapped in the cars. I'd peek up out of a backseat and see the Tuckers huffing from the gas tank at the corner of the lot. They'd put some in a mayonnaise jar and put their whole rat-nosed faces in the opening and breath in deep. Sometimes they all passed out, and I'd sneak inside and watch for the police to come. I never said a word, never moved from the back seat of that Bonneville, because the Tuckers lived right down the street and were a pair of crazy, mean, and stupid giants. And the Bonneville is probably where I got headlice.

By the time my mom finished combing the special shampoo though my hair, my scalp felt like meatloaf. She had on one of Dad's shirts from the refinery, and the smell of gasoline mixed with the chemicals of that shampoo almost made me faint.

My dad came home while I was drying my hair with a towel. He said, "Jesus, what stinks?" I could hear him taking off his clothes in the laundry room. The lice shampoo was so strong even he could smell it. My dad lost his sense of smell.

He came in the bathroom wearing nothing but his BVDs. He turned his back on me and dropped them an inch. Then he looked over his shoulder at Mom and me, bent at the middle, and farted. Then he got in the shower and tossed them out on to the linoleum floor.

By the time he came out of the bathroom with a towel wrapped around his middle, whistling "Pop Goes the Weasel," the only song he ever whistled, Ma was bawling. He asked her "What's the matter with you?"

She stood quivering. I pretended to watch TV. She said, "Jesus Christ, David!"

He said, "Honey?"

She said, "I spend my whole goddam life trying to give that boy something better, but I don't see why. Not with the example you set. He's got head lice, for Christ's sake. Goddam headlice!" She was red in the face, and her fists were balled by her side.

He said, "You got a better idea of where I should work, I'm all ears." They fought a lot because Dad worked ten hours a day and went out three nights a week. Dad more or less always assumed this defense even before he knew what they were going to fight about, to the point that it had become a joke. He grinned. It drove Ma nuts.

She said, "That's not what I'm talking about."

He said, "What? Me farting? Come on!" He laughed, stood on one leg, and farted again. She threw the candy dish at the floor, and it rolled to the wall. I was just getting ready to bolt up the stairs, when Dad looked me in the eyes. He said, "We better get out of here, doncha think?" He went to the laundry room and got some clothes.

We got in Dad's big brown Impala. We called it the Steaming Brown Pile when ma wasn't around. He turned it over and waited for the backfire. He cranked the country station up and we rode out to the Kinzu Dam.

The stars were out and I contemplated everything I did not yet know. I did not know that the shoulder on the left is where I'd be picked up, years later, for my first DUI. I didn't know when we passed the Rathskeller that I'd lose my bouncing job there because it would have violated my probation. I didn't know that some day I'd be a grown man and see my ma, older but still thin, happier, dancing with a short man in boots at the Texan in Erie, or that I'd see them kiss tenderly at the end of a Vince Gill slow number. I didn't know then, as we passed the fairgrounds, that I would some day meet Kenny Rogers at the Holiday Inn Lounge the year he played the Warren County Fair. I didn't know any of this. Then it was just dark and scary wonder.

Dad said, "Pull my finger."

I said, "Huh?"

He said, "Pull my finger."

I said, "That's an old one. Roll down your window."

All of a sudden he sounded like he was begging. He said, "C'mon! Pull it. Please?"

I looked at his hand, the long dirty index finger pointing out in to space. I gave it a tug. Dad's ass vibrated against the vinyl seat, and the whole car stank instantly, like a stable. He looked at me and grinned. "Hormel chili for lunch." He made a V with his fingers. He said, "Two whole cans!" His face grew restful and he turned around and headed for home.

It was school rules that I had to take two days off, and Ma washed my hair with that terrible stuff three times each day. I took the bad with the good, like Dad always said, and snuck out to the Bonneville both days. I took Ma's book with me, the one with the picture of the Arab and the sexy redhead. On the second day Ma caught me. She saw me from the upstairs window. I'd forgotten she was cleaning the blinds. The blinds upstairs were usually pulled closed. Ma hated to catch even a little glimpse of the junkyard. Next to Dad and me, she said it was the central pain of her life. She complained about it all the time. She was always asking Dad why we couldn't have normal neighbors like decent people. Dad just said a junkyard doesn't have loud parties. What more did she want?

She said, softly, "So that's where you've been." I felt myself get so hot I figured I'd turn purple. My eyes darted around the room for someplace to hide. She said, pleading, "I better not ever see you near those filthy cars again, you hear me, young man?

I said, "Yup."

She said, "I've told you a thousand times."

I said, "Yup."

She said, quiet as a mouse, "I can't believe you're my son. I can believe you're your father's boy, there's no question. But I can't believe you're my son." It was weird, her not yelling like that. She just looked at me. Then it got really weird. She said, "It's as strange as being married to trash like your father. I might as well have stayed on Daddy's farm slopping hogs for cleaning up after you two." Then she started crying.

That part wasn't true. My grandpa didn't have a hog farm. I

don't know where she got that. He raised corn and apples and chickens, and bred Rottweiler dogs with an AKC license and everything. But no pigs.

I said, "I can just go watch TV instead."

She said, "Do that." Then she stared over my head, out the window. She didn't want to look at me.

She didn't say a word when my dad got home, and didn't look at either of us once over dinner. People say that, she didn't even look at me, but I mean it. Dad stuck out his tongue and rolled his eyes and snorted like he was coughing something up. He told a joke about a Pollack. I told him he was a Pollack, and he said I was a Pollack. He blew his nose loudly in his napkin. He even got up and mooned her. She didn't budge.

After dinner dad and me watched Dukes. Ma sat in her rocker reading a book called A Knight of Desire. She was wearing a long dress and had her feet curled up under her butt. The picture on the book showed a man in armor holding a girl in his arms. The girl had huge boobs and long blond hair, and her dress was coming undone.

Dad got off the couch and sat down on the floor. He looked up at her for a while. Then, real soft, he said, "That's about the prettiest girl I've ever seen."

Ma turned the book over and looked at the cover. She said, "It's easy to be pretty when you don't exist. When you're not real, you can be anything at all." Then she got up and went to her bedroom.

He yelled after her, "Honey, I wasn't talking about no book!" but she didn't answer. I tried to take off for bed before Dad could suggest going for a ride. I didn't get far.

We rode up through Allegheny National Forest with the sun turning red as it started to set. Dad turned the radio on to the country station and more-or-less whistled "Pop Goes the Weasel" along with Kenny Rogers' "The Gambler." Don't ask me how he did it. He said, "Red skies at morning, sailors take warning. Red skies at night, sailors delight." He said it like he wasn't saying it to anyone in particular. The woods looked nice, green after being buried under snow for so long. When it was almost dark he stopped the car and said, "Get out."

I said, "Huh?"

He said, "You heard me, cootie boy. I don't want no cootie boy riding in my Steaming Brown Pile. Your mama doesn't want no cootie boy in her nice clean palace, either."

I said, "Huh?"

He said, "Get moving!"

I couldn't believe it. I opened my door and got out. An owl screeched somewhere out in the forest. I looked at my dad's serious eyes as he watched me. Then he said, "Can't have a cootie boy in your ma's palace."

I said, "How'm I supposed to get home?"

He said, "That, luckily, is not my concern. Close your door." His eyes were wild and stern at the same time.

I was about to cry, but I did as I was told. I didn't want to get tailed, and I prayed that this was just one of his jokes. When I slammed the door, dad started laughing. I didn't care much about the head lice. They didn't itch or anything. But I didn't feel all that great about it either, especially the idea that word would get around the eighth grade at St. Cecilia's eventually, and then the whole town. I was going to be in some fights, I knew that much. People already thought I was dirty. I opened the door and got back in.

Dad was still laughing his ass off. He said, "Boy, I had you going, didn't I? Didn't I? Didn't I, cootie boy? Cootie-pie? Crazy Cootie-er!" This set him off laughing again, and he wiped his eyes before he put the car back in gear. He kept giggling all the way home. He was a good father. He tried hard. It just wasn't all that funny.

When we got there all the drapes were taken down and the washing machine was running. Ma was in her bedroom with the door locked and the little TV in there turned all the way up. It sounded like English people.

Dad said, "Looks like I'm taking the couch. Want to watch some late-night cable?"

I could tell he really wanted company. When she turned the cold shoulder on him, he always seemed broken and lost. I said no. I'd had about enough of my dad. I went to bed.

It was all the junkyard's fault, I knew that: the dirt and grime, the lice, all of it. The junkyard was worse than my dad's oily smell, his jokes, the cars he drove. In the bible it says two things: the "wages of sin is death," which means anything bad you do comes back to haunt you, and that thing about if a part of your body makes you sin, cut it off. It applies to things that are bad influences. I knew what I had to do.

It took me all afternoon. First I got a mop bucket out of the basement. I filled it up part way with gasoline from the tank, and carried it all over the junkyard. I poured two buckets' worth through the windows of both the VW and the Bonneville. I poured it over the tops of all the wrecks. I sloshed more buckets than I can count on that hateful eyesore of a pile of tires, with its mosquito hatcheries and rotting rubber smell. I soaked the ripped red ragtop of an old rusted-out MG, an English car you never see one on the road up here. I soaked its moldy sheepskin seat covers. Gasoline pooled under and around the cars, and made rainbows in the puddles. No one noticed because sometimes the whole town stunk like gasoline, because everybody except the husbands of the women my ma wanted so desperately to be friends with worked at the refinery, at least since Nichol's Sheetmetal closed. I emptied that tank.

I didn't think it was going to catch at first. I lit a box of kitchen matches and pitched it at the MG. The box sat there, and seemed to go out. I was just about to go back in and light it again when the box flared up. There was a minute when the matches cast shadows across the hills and valleys of the ragtop. Then it erupted like a volcano. The flames jumped up around the Bonneville, then jumped from one car to the next, spreading out in broken waves. I took off for the bushes across the street. I couldn't help but watch. The whole junkyard caught fire, and a plume of thick oily smoke came from the tires. It stank to high heaven. A gas tank popped. I heard the big siren calling the firefighters, but knew they'd be too late. Nothing could stop that fire. The heat from the fire was my mother's love coming back to everything, to everyone. It was a night in a log cabin with mom and dad kissing and hugging on the couch until it was time for me to go to bed, early, so that they could get in some nookie, which would have been fine with me. It was a holy fire that would leave my father a man with a nice house by an empty lot. I thought without the temptation of the cars, I would be a new boy, maybe a man. And I figured maybe Dad, deprived of its evil presence, would grow like the lilacs Ma planted to fill the empty space in the fence. Empty space, like a blank page. The junkyard was history, the cars useless even for parts. It was like I was an ant crawling around a campfire. I could feel the heat from it. Flames curled and rolled like dolphins in a blender.

Then I noticed my mistake. The wind was blowing harder, damp and a little cool. And the fence between my house and the junkyard was on fire.

It occurred to me that I probably had about as much chance of making my ma happy as Dad did, which was none at all.

By the time the volunteer fire company got organized and pulled in with sirens crying and lights flashing, the house was completely on fire. So was the sycamore in the front yard.

People came from all over town as the junkyard finished burning (all except for the tire dump, which burned for a solid month) and our house shrank from a tower of flame to a wet black pit between the front and back yards.

I got four years probation and a court order saying I couldn't get my driver's license until I was eighteen. And I had to go talk to Melvin Tasker the therapist about my pyromania twice a week for a year. That was the deal. My ma moved in with her cousin Lynnie. We stayed out at a cabin my dad looked after for a guy who lived in Pittsburgh. My dad went alone to talk to Nick from the Texaco, and to the District Attorney Bill Sweet (Ma worshipped his wife, Candis Sweet), and to Sheriff Buza. My dad quit making dumb jokes to Mr. Sweet when the bald old man asked him if he wanted his boy to go to juvenile hall because he was a jackass. But the cops loved him. He had them busting their guts for two hours solid.

Ma and me didn't talk much. When I'd see her in town, she didn't have much to say to me. Why would she? Having a son who was already kicked out of Catholic school for being a danger to the other students, and who was now trying not to have to go to jail ruined my ma's chances of fitting in to her social circle, and Warren was too small a town to keep anything a secret. It didn't help that I couldn't bear to be around her, to see her.

We ran in to Ma outside the Bi-Lo. She had a small bag of groceries. She barely said hello to my dad, but she looked right at me and smiled. I could feel the days without showers, feel the way my hair was standing up on my head. I stammered. I felt like I had to pee. I wanted to throw my arms around her, and I wanted to bolt in the other direction.

I had advertised my foolishness in giant flaming letters, and Ma saw.

I did nothing. I just stood there until she went on her way.

After about a month of cooking Spaghetti-O's on a pot-bellied stove, and pissing in the woods, and moving from smelly to rancid and then to what Dad said was "an attractive manly musk," I missed her like a madman. I would walk in the door of the cabin and expect to see her. Sometimes I cried when Dad was at work. I wished I was a baby again, and she would hold me close to her. Then Dad came in one night and dangled a ring of keys that sparkled in the bare bulb from the ceiling.

We rode out to the Forrest Campgrounds, which was a mobile home park. Dogs were chained to the cinderblocks that supported rows of doublewides. Flowers bloomed in boxes. We got to our trailer around nine at night, and he fixed some cans of beans and weenies on the little stove. It was easy to see that Ma wasn't there. The curtains were filthy. He put the steaming plate of beans in front of me. What I wanted was Ma's pork roast. I said, "Nice place."

He said, "It ain't your ma's palace, but it's home."

I said, "Is she coming back? Is she coming here?"

We sat for a moment. I looked at him across the yellow formica of the table. I watched little spasms cross his face. He looked back towards me, over my head. He said, "Jesus, but do you have too much of your mother in you." He looked back down at the top of the table. He said, "Why don't you go in and watch Dukes."

I got up and walked to the couch, a big flowered thing. I sat down and smelled dog right away. There was no TV. I knew this, and I also knew that my dad knew this. It was a joke.

So I watched my father sit at the table. Later in life, I knew what I saw in him and felt myself was impotence and grief. He picked at the aluminum edging. His face worked as he tried to decipher the patterns on the vinyl in front of him. Then he screwed up his face, farted, and howled at the rising moon.

Even the Dust

Dick tossed his cigarette butt out the window. He inhaled deeply, the rank smell of raw sewage filling the cab of his truck as we squinted in the glare and crossed the bridge. He said, "Ah, New Jersey," and laughed.

We took I95 down along the river past the airport and got off in Eddystone. I was quiet. I'd lost my job, and Dick was throwing me some laborer's stuff, some nasty, dirty under-the-table demolition work in an abandoned foundry. There were chemicals involved—a huge, terrifying plastic tank bearing a sign in red foot-high letters (DANGER ACID), buckets and bins of caustics, black barrels marked with ominous symbols. And marijuana flowing through us like the lie that adversity makes you stronger. We were strong. The first hit of the day is sometimes the most important.

The foundry was ice cold and musty. We spent a few minutes stretching and drinking Cokes. I was wearing longjohns and layers of clothes, but the morning air sent fingers through me. I hated what lay ahead: the taste of drywall, the numbness of arms vibrated by power tools, the sickening ozone of a Sawzall held at precarious angles, eyes red with sweat, shitting in toilets that hadn't been cleaned in ten years. I wanted my shitty old job back, my shitty old life back home. I got tricked into a promotion 300 miles away from Pittsburgh, only to find that my new boss was looking at a fat bonus if she could turn me out quickly. We played cat and mouse for a while, and then Cadence nailed me because I lost my girlfriend and went crazy. With no woman and no job I got crazier. Dick liked the change. He wanted me to work this job, take the cash, sell my car, buy an old Dodge panel van and set out on the American Tour. He was sure it was the best thing for me to do, the best thing for anyone. I thought about vandalizing Cadence's car, about waiting late at night to shoot the evil bitch in the head. I prayed for unemployment. I didn't sleep. I started smoking again. I lay awake and dreamed of cancer. I wished that the pain inside of me would jump up and throttle me; I was calling its bluff.

We worked all day, stapling plastic sheets to walls, cutting out copper pipe, watching the soles of our work boots begin to melt in the ooze that covered some of the floors. That was the idea: industrial waste cleanup on the cheap. They weren't going to do anything with the building because, over a dozen reincarnations, it had acquired the sludge of a dozen toxic industries. "Make it look neat," the guy had said. Even the dust frightened me.

And the fucking tank of acid. We had a warm day, and the whole place smelled of it, our eyes stung. The money wasn't just good; it was all we could find in March. A few months later we could have cut lawns six days a week and blown it all on Corona and Mexican brown.

We worked quietly, but there were outbursts. Dick surprised me with the pressure washer, trying to clear the muck from my Tyvek suit, and hit me in the balls. I went down on one knee. He couldn't stop laughing, and, eventually, neither could I.

We bought Polish sausage sandwiches with brown mustard from the roach coach that still sailed the complex, and we ignored the shit all over our hands when we ate. Dick showed me how to use the butcher paper that came wrapped around our sandwiches so I didn't have to touch anything I put in my mouth. We made jokes: "Hey, Cliff, wouldn't you like to send Cadence for a swim in the big vat of acid?" We named that fear: the Vat of Acid, something from the horror film that our lives were becoming. Dick was cheating on disability doing this job, and his hands were claws frozen on the steering wheel as we drove home at night. I was three hundred miles from home, broke, unemployed, alone. We decided we'd wear dime-store red-devil costumes and black leotards, play the theme from The Addams Family over and over, suspend her from the ceiling by a rope, pare it down strand by strand with a Buck knife.

Cadence, my old boss, became someone for him to blame,

too.

We tore out wire and drop ceilings, light fixtures and air conditioners. We used a pressure-washer to scrub everything that might be sold later. I climbed ladders and used a Sawzall upside-down. I choked on the dust.

When I thought of the woman I lost I could do those things. When I thought of April, curly red hair and hot freckled skin, I had just enough courage to stand in front of a locomotive.

We worked on fixtures one day. There was a heat exchanger hanging from the ceiling, a quarter ton of steel. Dick was cutting with the Sawzall, and I was on the short ladder, holding the thing, feeling the mad vibration of all of those pipes, that steel. The leg came off my ladder, just below the bottom rung. Dick shouted. I pushed myself backwards, the enormous manifold swaying on the tow strap supporting it. I hit a steel support and then the ground. I held my head. I heard Dick's voice. I looked up at the swaying steel. I wondered if it would fall and crush me. I looked at it coming a little closer, going a little farther away, and wondered. I scuttled backwards as it rocked. My heart was beating.

"Cliff?"

"I'm okay," I said. "You okay?"

He rounded the corner, picked up the remains of the wooden ladder with one hand, and threw it outside. I sat in sawdust and filings on the cool floor, feeling the bruised but whole bones of my hands, legs, neck, arms, back. He jumped on the ladder. He kicked it with his boots, brown leather opalescent with accidents of chemistry. He swung it against the wall of the building. He looked at me.

Dick loved me, completely and without reservation; he called me "brother" sometimes. He was my oldest friend, a felon and a sociopath, the boy who invented Baby Bird Season and taught me to hunt groundhogs with a Volkswagen, the young barbarian who introduced me to drugs. I once watched him pull a treble hook out of his scalp, and he only seemed puzzled by the blood that soaked his hair and ran down his forehead. People were scared of him.

He said, "I taught that fucker a lesson."

I nodded and tried to light a cigarette. I was shaking. A truck shifted gears out on the highway. There were no birds. There was lichen growing in a crack in the asphalt, a gray-green fault. Dick put his hands over my fist. He struck the lighter and guided the flame to my cigarette. "Hey buddy," he said softly. "That was a good fall; you kept your head up."

He sat down and lit a cigarette. He looked out over the lot. A wide muddy puddle lay like a moat before the concrete steps. The wind kicked up grit that hissed against the corrugated sides of the next building. He said, "Feel good to be alive?" and we sat listening to someone testing helicopter turbines up at Boeing. After a while, we collected our tools, locked the place up. We walked to the truck in silent agreement: fuck Eddystone. Fuck this job.

Driving back across the bridge, the winter sunlight pale and the arc of the bridge carrying us toward it, we smelled the sewage, and Dick said, "Welcome to Philthadelphia," while I cried and he looked away.

Ilka, Ilse, Kostas and Pie

You get some people in this country, they are afraid of everything foreign, they so stupid they think socialism is the same thing as communism. Like the damn Texans. They sell their water company to a business and you know what they pay? The man was on TV, he paid twelve hundred a month. For water. They vote for that, then they gonna cry about it. Dummkopfs. Float them all in the ocean on a raft and sink it. Who needs 'em?

I can't talk to everybody. When you work with the public you have toyou have to put on a face and take a lot of crap from some people. Some people around here. They are not educated, and it makes a person mean. The café across the street, we tell people to go over there when we are too full up. I tell them they have a good sandwich. You know what he does? The guy who owns it? Two of my regular customers—you know we closed on Tuesdays? Two ladies come to my place every day, and they go to him on Tuesday, and one day he says to them, what I gotta do to get you to come here every day? They such good customers, they go to Dunkin Donuts on Tuesday now! Some people are just terrible. Terrible. We all having trouble. It's so hard right now, but we ought to stick together, merchants, not stick the knife in the other's back.

The place we had in Hamilton years ago, we made more money on eight stools and a counter than we do here, any day. I used to get up at three in the damned morning. I make the muffins and the desserts. I do an apple and raisin pie. Word got around, and the guy comes in, says he heard we have a pie she makes like a strudel. No time, I sell ten of those a day, every day of the week. Here, I make them, a guy asks me what the raisins are, shit? I says, you think I put shit in my food, you get out and don't come back neither. And I said I was never gonna make them again, but I lied and a couple years ago I made two of them and they sold right out. But I used to do all that, and then I told him, I ain't going to do it anymore. The whole thing was his dream, not mine, and I ain't getting up at three o'clock in the morning for him no more.

This one back here, my Kostas, he's a bastard. I can't hardly stand him. He's a bully. He clicks clicks clicks, you want to watch this, you want to watch that. I'm seventy-eight years old, I don't wanna watch that bullshit. I like to go outside. I walk, I look at the ducks. We go to Bradley Palmer Park but he don't go. You know, I walk a while, but I don't just walk, I stop and look at things. I look at birds, clouds, trees. You need it. Not this one. He just sits and sits. I only stayed with him because I already had one daughter, was already divorced, and I wanted Ilse to grow up with a father. That was part of it.

I wished I'd gone home. I only came to this damned country for my education, because the university was out of this world, but when I got here, I can't afford and I never got my Master's degree. Engineer, I was going to be. I don't know why I didn't go home. My mother and my brother, they both say, you'll come home in tears, and I don't want to go home in tears so I stayed.

My other daughter—her father was a one hundred percent kraut, and she's a kraut through and through. She hears a joke and I gotta explain it to her, and then she laughs. She was born deaf, and the one time we take her to the St. Francis School, you know, for the deaf up here, and the nuns say they don't have no place for her. And what the hell I'm gonna do? Her smart as a whip and can read lips, but she needed the education. And what do you know, Mr. Winthrop, he knows the bishop, and he comes to the house and takes us up there, and he says to the nuns to meet my daughter, and she goes up and she curtsies! And the nun, she takes her in just like that, says we need to have this girl at our school because she's brought up so good.

But Mr. Winthrop, I didn't know he spoke German! He come in every day with his, whatchacallit, little suitcase and his hat, and every day it's coffee and a muffin, coffee and a muffin, and he don't smile or look at me. So the one day, I says under my breath in German, If you smiled your face would fall right off, and he shoots right back in German and he says, All you krauts are all the same. And I was so embarrassed, but after that he smiled and met my eye and he was a gentleman.

This daughter who works here, she does all kind of shit, and Kostas don't get mad. So I guess I did that right, anyway. But he was an awful bastard. There was this one son of a bitch who used to come in and sit at the counter, and he would tell me I should get down on my knees and thank my husband for taking me out of Germany after the war. And I would get so awful mad I like to punch him in the eye. Kostas thought it was funny, but the one day I had enough. So the son of a bitch says to me how lucky I am Kostas took me out of Germany after the war, and I yell at Kostas, you know that ain't how it was, you bastard, why don't you stand up for me? Because my mother's side was Jewish. My grandfather died in the camps, but after the war they made a textile factory and it was good money. And Kostas, he just laughs. And so I take off my apron, and I say I'm going home, and I ain't getting up at three o'clock no more, and you can just buy the muffins from a bakery. I tell him this is your dream, not mine. And I never did get my Masters degree that I was supposed to get.

I should have married Isaac Edelstein, from Pittsburgh. Nice Jewish boy. He was my love. But he was there, and I was up here, and it just stopped. What are you gonna do? I make the trip, but it was too far. So, what am I gonna do? Nothing.

Ach, a guy one time says all you do in Massachusetts is complain. I tell him at least we don't shoot nobody.

Seventy-Two-Pound Fish Story

I walked in to the kitchen and announced to my dad that I was changing my name to Amazing Popeil, after the inventor of the Popeil's Pocket Fisherman—I had made up my mind once and for all, and there was nothing he could do about it. He glanced at me and then went back to watching the TV news. I stood there for a while. He looked back and smiled his please-go-away-it's-too-early-for-this-shit smile.

I said, "I'll do it! I will! I'll run away and join Bassmasters."

He got mad. I knew better than to disturb him while he was working up his general outrage at the world to go to the plant and be a good supervisor. He was having a big mug of coffee and a bottle of Maalox for breakfast. I knew I'd picked a bad time to pitch a fit, Mandatory Overtime Saturday, but I was desperate. It was a hot day already, and I knew the fish would be crammed in close under every bit of shade, that they'd be mad and slow, grabbing at each other with cold heavy lips, that they wouldn't be biting. I didn't care. I didn't know this because I was some kind of fisherman. I didn't know it because I was a fisherman's son. I knew it because I watched Bassmasters every Sunday morning at six in exactly the same way my Nana went to church. I'd spent every penny of three years worth of birthday money on tackle. I had flies, lures, worms in a wooden box in the shade by the garage, waiting, ready. I had a Zebco rod and two kinds of reels. I had a magic potion Nana got from the TV that was supposed to send bass into a feeding frenzy. I had a deep lust in my heart for the wide slow Perkiomen Creek and everything that swam between her banks. I was ten years old and had never been fishing.

Dad said, "Is this about fishing again?"

"Duh!"

He said, "Just for that, we're not going, smart-ass" in the tone he saved for when he thought he was out-smarting me.

I was desperate. I yelled, "Call me Amazing Popeil from now on" in a voice that shook the house and opened up the clouds.

My dad said, "Jesus. I give up."

Surprised, a deep and satisfying peace settled over me, the peace I imagined feeling on a boat, with a line dangling over the side, wearing a good hat, and eating peanut butter sandwiches. I always fell for it.

He said, "One day soon we'll get out there and catch some fish."

I gave up. I drained away.

Two weeks later my dad woke me up at four on Saturday morning. I looked at him through the crusty sleep in my eyes. He said, "Get up. You're going fishing."

I figured it was a hoax. I tried to lie back down. But his words were solid in the room, breathing all the air. I jumped straight up, put on my Phillies hat, and pulled up my jeans. I grabbed my toolbox full of gear and my Zebco rod in its nylon case. I limped out the front door, dreamed happily that we would soon be father and son, alone for the day, fishing. Dad was in the truck. He was wearing brown pants and a brown shirt, and his hair wasn't combed. His spare tire bulged over his belt. His face was half shaven, and Maalox crusted the stubble at the corners of his mouth. He said, "Took you long enough."

I settled in, then looked around. I said, "What are you going to do for a rod?" I suddenly had a horrifying vision of my dad sitting peaceful and happy in the stern of a rowboat, with my brand new Zebco rod in his fat hands, slowly sipping at a blue plastic bottle of antacid, while I looked on, powerless.

He looked at me like I was nuts, then went back to driving.

We met Luther Gorman at the Valley Diner at four-thirty. He had his son Alec with him. Alec was two years older than me, and what everyone called "slow"; we were in the same grade at St. Cecilia's. His forehead was large and square, like his mother's.

Mr. Gorman was a tall thin man with a bald spot that covered the whole top of his head except for a thin ring of hair at the front, which he left long and combed back. He was a salesman for a uniform company. My dad had met him at work. They shook hands stiffly.

I went to put my things in the back of Mr. Gorman's station wagon, but he said, "That rod won't do you any good. We're going sea fishing. That's too light."

I looked at my precious rod in its case, a one-stringed magic harp singing to be played, felt the ridges of the rough nylon compartments where each segment lay slick and ready. I said, "On a boat?"

"Sure, on a boat," he said.

I put my gear back in Dad's truck. Dad gave me two twenty dollar bills, which I stared at as if he'd filled my hand with hard round sheep turds.

I said, "You're not coming?" I looked at the Gormans, their quietude, their dingy clothes and rattletrap car, and was afraid. I didn't know what I'd talk to them about. I didn't know how I'd explain, for the nine-millionth time in my short life, why I was alone in a place with men and their sons. I always felt the accusing eyes of those men on me, read in myself what I was sure they could see, a boy whose father didn't even want to be around him, a momma's boy, a boy that would never be a man, that didn't hunt, or fish, or play ball, or go camping. I knew they could tell and it always made me ashamed.

Dad laughed like it was the craziest thing he'd heard all week, and got back in his truck.

By the time the sun came up, we had crossed the New Jersey state line. Alec said, "He's awake, Daddy."

Mr. Gorman said, "Hey there, Amazing."

I said, "Huh?"

He said, "Your pop said you liked to be called Amazing Popeil. S'at right?"

I wasn't sure if he was laughing at me or humoring me. I figured he was humoring me. I figured I was so troubled, crazy in fact, to fish that it showed. I figured he saw my dad's neglect written on the skin of my face, and he pitied me. I figured if anyone was laughing at me, it was my own dad. I said, "That's right."

I felt naked and lonely, riding in the strange old car. Mr. Gorman smoked one Camel after another with the windows up, the old car's air conditioner barely keeping the heat at bay.

He said, "Well, Alec says you two know each other from school, and since we're fishing I think you can call me Lute."

I said, "Okay Lute." I liked the sound of the grown-up man's first name as I said it. My voice sounded deep. I said it again: "Lute."

He said, "Huh?"

"Uh, nothing," I said.

"Oh." He said, "Your daddy says you've never been fishing."

I felt cold then hot. My entire life was one long whine, begging to be taken to a creek, a pond, a river, and I was embarrassed by it, and more embarrassed that I had never done it, smelling the smoke and greasy odors in the car. I wondered for a split second if I was the butt of a joke, and then decided Lute didn't know anything, and I didn't want him to know anything. I couldn't picture my dad's face if I closed my eyes. I never saw him, except for a couple of minutes at a time. I couldn't explain it. I said, "First time deep sea fishing. My dad and me go fishing all the time. I just guess he had something to do."

"Oh," he said. "Oh. I must've got that wrong. You'll like deep sea fishing. We try to go as often as I'm home and can get away."

I looked at Alec. His permanent caveman frown clashed with his wide grin. I looked back at the road.

Lute said, "What do your pop and you go after?"

I said, "Trout and bass, mostly. Bluegill. Sometimes we go for catfish, but dad doesn't like to eat them."

He said, "Me neither. But they're fun to catch."

"Yeah," I said.

"Yeah," he said. Alec kept on grinning.

By seven I'd coughed up most of the forty bucks for boat fee and rod rental and bait and breakfast, which was Coke and butterscotch TastyKakes. Lute and Alec had season passes from the charter company and their own rods. The boat stank of fish and men and diesel fuel. Paint peeled from its sides in long strips. Rainbows hung in water so full of trash there wasn't room for fish to swim. Then the horn blasted, the engines surged, and I yacked over the rail of the boat. While I was yacking I heard men laughing, and I got hot and dizzy thinking they were laughing at me. I spit out the last of it and washed my mouth out with Coke. I spit over the side a couple more times. After a while the sun cut through the mist, and I got even dizzier. I tried to bait my hook, but I couldn't bring myself to touch the strips of squid. Lute did it for me, cast the hook overboard, and set the pole in my moist-plaster hands. I was defeated and angry. I looked at Alec, grinning, gripping his pole with both hands. I wanted to smack him. I said, "How's summer school Alec?"

He looked at me and said, "Not so bad." Alec went to summer school every year. It was widely known. Teachers got frustrated with him pretty often, and embarrassed him in class. One time Miss Bowdren made him suck his thumb. Bigger boys beat him up. He was always being sent to stand in the hall. I could get beaten up just for riding in his dad's car. I said, "Say hi to Eddie Sidlecki for me." Eddie did most of the beating up, and he went to summer school too. Alec's grin went away. I felt better.

Lute said, "What grade you in, Amazing?"

I said, "Sixth." Then I added, "But they're thinking of moving me up."

He said, "You should be proud of that."

I said, "I guess." I was a straight B and C student who had a hard time sitting still. I also tended to get other kids in trouble a lot.

He said, "What do you wanna be when you grow up?"

I said, "That's a tough one. I was thinking about being a doctor, a surgeon, but everyone says that would be a waste of my I.Q."

He looked out over the water.

I said, "I'm up over 300. They aren't supposed to show you that, you know, but they figured I ought to know. They keep saying I could graduate from college any time—take a test or something. But I just like to fish. Fish and go places with my dad." I tried to lean back on the thin plank seat, but after a minute I had to slump back down. I was hollow in my stomach, and the boat kept rocking.

"Doctor's a good job," he said. "Where do you and your dad fish?"

I had no idea. I'd been asking and asking, but I figured I'd leave that part up to him. I never believed I'd actually get to do it. I suddenly realized I was holding a thick fiberglass rod, with a reel as big as both my fists, strung with heavy monofilament line, baited with smelt and squid, a crescent of smoky land in the distance. Hungry monsters prowled the deep below. I thought quick. I said, "It's a secret. I'm not allowed to tell."

"Secret hole, huh." Lute spit over the rail in a perfect arc. "Must have pulled up a whale if it's that secret."

Aside, I whispered, "Seventy-two pounds." I gripped the rod tighter, held it straight.

"Wow, seventy-two-pound what?" he said, awed.

"It looked like a dinosaur," I said. I couldn't help it. Lute wouldn't shut up. Alec wouldn't speak. He was still reminding himself of what was waiting for him on Monday. Plus, I liked it, I liked the way Alec was looking at me. His dad was the one who had brought us here. Mr. Gorman seemed like he took Alec to a lot of places.

Once, my dad had to go to work every two hours, all night long, to meet a lady who was taking sound readings for the state because some neighbor lady had complained about the plant starting third shift. He took me along. Mostly I held stuff: coffee, flashlight, clipboard. I don't remember past four o'clock or so. Later, they said the crickets along his company's property line were louder than the noise from the factory. The lady who complained about the noise was a crank, and we'd done it all for nothing. Dad was pissed off for weeks afterwards. We hadn't been out alone together in the three years since then. I wanted to crawl up on Lute's lap and bury my face in his shirt, and I was disgusted by him. Dad didn't say anything to me that whole night, except, "Let's go." The look on Alec's face was envy. I wanted to see more of it.

"You don't know what kind you caught?" Lute said.

"I'm telling you, it was some kind of dinosaur, something prehistoric. We've been going after it for three years, trying to get another look. Something nobody's ever caught before. It snapped the line, but we saw it."

"How do you know it was seventy-two pounds if it snapped the line?" Lute said. He had a point. He was getting tired of me; it was something I was used to in adults. I'd been cranky all morning, and had barely looked at him the whole time. I couldn't remember ever getting up that early. I was hungry and queasy at the same time. I couldn't shut up.

I said, "My dad can estimate the weight of any fish to within three ounces." This was even better than the record of Lou Handie, American Champion Fish Weight Estimator, who'd been a special guest on Bassmasters once. I added, "Yeah. They once put him on a TV show for it."

"No kidding."

I looked at Alec, grimacing. I said, "Whatcha say there, Smart Alec?" This was something I'd heard both teachers and other kids call him. His eyes filled with tears. He looked down at his feet, seemed to pull up inside himself. I sat closer to Lute, almost against him.

I said, "Hey, Lute."

He said, "Why don't you call me Mr. Gorman, okay."

I couldn't think of anything to say anyway. So I sat there and fished.

We sat in the hazy sun for hours. All the peace and quiet drove me nuts. I got up and looked over the rail. I called "Heeeeeere fish" about six times. I could see several men nearby were annoyed. Lute said, "Shhhh. You'll scare them off. Pipe down. Have a seat."

I knew I'd displayed my ignorance again, that I'd been a pain in the ass all day. I didn't want to hang out with Luther Gorman or his idiot son. I wanted my dad. I said, in a voice loud enough for most of the men nearby to hear, "That's a myth, an old wives' tale. Experiments in Uganda have shown that fish respond to being called just like dogs." I picked Uganda because I always got it wrong on the maps in geography.

The man next to Lute, an older guy with thick tufts of ear hair and a half-shaven face, bent to look at me. His accent thick south-Philly, he said, "Hey. You. Effin' genius. Why don't you sit down. Now. And shut up." He turned back to fishing. I sat down and gripped my rod tighter.

Lute leaned over to the other man. He said, quietly, "Favor for a customer."

The old man nodded solemnly, understanding creased in his face. He said, "Christ what you have to do to make a buck." Clouds rolled in from the north.

When the rain started, I looked around. No one made a move to go inside. The men tied their poles to the rail and unfolded clear plastic ponchos. Lute and Alec put on theirs. I didn't have one. One of the guys who worked on the boat brought me a trash bag after a while, with holes for my head and arms, but I was already soaked through. Once in a long while someone would yell "NET!" and there'd be a little commotion. Otherwise the sky just got gradually darker, and it seemed like weeks went by like that, sitting in the rain under a wet Hefty bag and holding that stupid silent pole.

The rod bent and I clawed at the clutch to let out line. I almost lost the rig, and didn't have money to pay for it. I pulled back hard to set the hook, and the rod bent again. We fought for a few minutes, and Lute hollered for the net. I reeled in the slack, then let it out again when the fish surged. There seemed to be miles of line. The guy who'd given me the trash bag to wear came over and said, "Here, kid." He took my pole. I panicked.

I said, "MY fish!"

I needed to be the one that landed it. I had always needed to. My dad had made fun of my most precious and sacred desire for years. My whole life was hooked to that pole, my pride, my manhood, my future. I knew if I didn't do it myself I would end up teaching English instead of driving the big rigs. Tears filled my eyes, and I fought to keep from crying out. My feet begged to be stomped.

The net man said, "Sorry, kid. You hooked lines." He worked for a while to get us untangled, me and some guy on the other side of the boat. He said, "Lost your bait." I sighed, tried to keep from shivering. "We're moving the boat," he said. "You'll have better luck." I looked at him, wanting him to understand; I needed to show my dad a fish.

I stuck the hook through a thick strip of squid, then threaded it through the eye sockets of a smelt. I wrapped the white strip of squid around the baitfish as I'd seen the others do. I let out line and cast the hook as far from the boat as I could. I waited in my wet black Hefty bag, angry and determined.

When it struck, the line went out like a slow breath. I thought I felt something, but wasn't sure. I pulled to set the hook, and my line went slack. I started to reel back in, to check my bait, un-disappointed. I'd had a bite.

I'd only pulled in a few feet when the rod bent double and the reel began to whine. There were shouts all around me, "NET! NET!" Men croaked advice. Boys looked on in awe. I gave the fish line. A man who smelled like woodsmoke kneeled down behind me and held me to the floor, his arms clenched around my chest. Another man gripped the rod above my hands so I could work the reel. Far out to sea, the fish jumped. We pulled and reeled. I forgot about being wet, about the burning in all my muscles. Men everywhere were shouting "Amazing! That's Amazing!" cheering for me. It was enormous, a sea bass someone said, close to seventy pounds, the best anyone had gotten all day. I had landed it. It broke the line just as it was scooped in the net. It filled the mesh. Two men were hauling it in, and the man who'd been holding my waist held me up over the rail so I could see. It was hoary and gorgeous, curled like a cat, sparkling in the dim lights from the boat. The wind sluiced rain against us. And then as quickly as it had fallen in to the net, the net went overboard, the fish along with it.

Everyone apologized and slapped me on the back, tough luck. I said, "I don't care," looking after the fish in to the waters of the Atlantic Ocean, and I didn't. I'd caught a monster. I was a fisherman. I had nothing to worry about. I saw a vision of myself, broad and strong and good looking, with a booming voice, speaking into a microphone, holding a crowd in my sway.

Alec slept against me in the car. I didn't mind. Mr. Gorman played the oldies station. When I started talking to him, he turned it up louder. I went to sleep, smelling fish all over the car.

I woke up a few miles from town when Alec jumped up and yelled "HOME!" I was stiff and groggy. We pulled in to my driveway, and Mr. Gorman blew his horn.

Dad came out the front door and hustled up the walk. He was

still in his work clothes. Mr. Gorman jumped out of the car and ran to meet him.

"How's it going Gorman?"

"Fine, just fine."

My dad looked down at me. He said, "Did you catch anything?"

I said, "Yeah, but the boat guys lost it in the net."

Mr. Gorman snapped his head around sideways to look at me. Dad didn't notice. He said, "Well, good."

Mr. Gorman said, "So when can we get together to talk shop?" He smiled a wide Vaseline smile I had not seen before. My dad pulled out his pocket calendar and started to look it over. I said, "It was huge, dad. It was the biggest fish anyone caught all day. Everyone was cheering." He was looking at his pocket calendar. My voice rose in pitch and volume and desperation. "They all said I was a natural fisherman. I landed it myself, except for the net guys. They lost it. I fought it for hours. Everyone thought I'd have to give up. I was weak from hunger and thirst. The wind was blowing. Rain slapped against us and the boat rocked. But I caught it. I caught it."

Mr. Gorman looked over at me crossly, then back at my dad with his Vaseline smile. He said, "Yeah, that boy is some fisherman." He looked back at me without his smile. He said, "That thing must have weighed seventy-two pounds. I'm pretty good at estimating, you know, and that fish weighed seventy-two pounds if it was an ounce. Your boy's got quite a fish story. Now when's good for you?"

My dad looked over his calendar, held it with his thumb, moved it so Mr. Gorman couldn't see. He ruled out one day after another. Finally, he said, "Listen, I'll get back to you. Soon. We'll get this taken care of soon." He slipped his calendar back in his pocket. Mr. Gorman, slumped down, kept his Vaseline smile, and said his good-byes. Alec got in the front seat of his car. I looked back at them, talking close, huddled together in the waning light. Then they backed away. They didn't wave.

I followed dad up the walk. He said, "Sounds like you had a fun day."

I said, "Yeah, it was the best. It was the best day of my life."

"Sounds wonderful," he said.

"We saw dolphins and seals. One man caught a giant lobster. But not as big as my fish. Everyone kept patting me on the back, saying my old man must be proud of me."

He said, "That sounds great. I'm sorry I missed it." He stopped, turned, and looked at me.

I said, "Me too."

He said, "We should do that. We should go fishing. Soon."

"Soon," I said. We'll definitely go do it soon.

Bridgeville

It was the summer before Jack's dad lost his job and had to sell the camp up near Lake Sharon, with its wood-fired cookstove and bunk beds, and they had been alone for most of the month of August there. He was going into his last year of high school, and she was going away to college at the end of the month. They made a point to make love in every room, like vandals, screwing on the cold iron stove, the smooth butcherblock counters, the picnic table in the yard, on the old Jetski, in the rowboat, and twice, at least, on every bed. They filled ashtray after ashtray with butts, smoked joints, and drank whiskey from his dad's stash in the hiding place bootleggers had made under the kitchen floor in the twenties. Meaghan was thirteenth in her class of nearly 600, and she would lie next to him and talk about college, and about things she read.

Jack liked Star Trek, so she told him about the stars, about Chinese astrology, about probability, and myth. He swooned when she got that way, and curled like a baby against her and slept so deeply he seemed not to breathe. Jack's mother had been 16 when Randall, her first, was born. When he mentioned it one night as they lay together, Meaghan said "Don't worry. The pill is way better nowadays."

The cabin had a little TV, and Jack brought a miniature satellite dish he had scavenged, part by part, from the high school. He was in occupational education, in the electronics, telecommunications and avionics program, and he was the unofficial editor of the yearbook video, so he had keys to the studio, the a/v lab, and the server closet. Meaghan liked shows about magical women, and she said she got turned on watching

Xena: Warrior Princess, so he sat through it, even though he preferred the scientific-sounding explanations for events he could count on to make science fiction seem real. Dilithium crystals, warp factors, Magellanic clouds, the perfume of her long dark hair, her mouth and hands and arching back.

On rainy days they went through his collection of videotapes over and over. She liked the scene in The Doors where the sexy witch traces spells on Jim Morrison's body, and she did this when they lay coiled together, first with her finger and later with poster paint, ice cubes, a dull kitchen knife, and an extra-wide Sharpie. She said she was binding him to her, so that they'd always have this perfect love. He said, "You own me" and she kissed him sweetly and said, "I know."

The night before they were to head home, they sat in the dark of a willow looking out at the stars reflected on Lake Sharon. Night birds called out on the far shore, and Meaghan leaned back against him, filling his view with curls and his whole being with the syrup smell of sunblock. She said, "Do you now how long it takes the light from those stars to reach the earth?"

He said, "Around seventy million years?"

She turned around and looked at him, her features hidden in shadow. He could feel her eyes, and he didn't know what she wanted. After a few moments she said, "You think you aren't smart, but you are."

He said, "I just know stuff like that from watching the Sci Fi channel. And from hanging around with Jeremy."

She turned around and pressed her face to his shoulder. "You are too smart," she said. "I mean, I really feel like I'm an open book resting in your lap. And your best friend wants to be a physicist. How does that add up to not smart?"

"We just, like, hang out. Bust on each other, play his Nintendo. We don't talk about physics. I don't know anything about physics."

He put his hand on her collarbone, his fingers tracing her throat, pulling curls straight and letting them bounce back. Almost moonless, the darkness was blue, and he suddenly felt protective of her so that every shape and shadow seemed like something lying in wait to snatch her away; thinking about eyes in the darkness gave him the willies, and she pulled herself up to look at him as he shook them off.

"Sorry," he said. "I just talked myself into the dark creeping me out." She sniffed, and he knew she had been crying. He bent forward and kissed the tears from her cheeks until she grabbed his shirt and kissed his mouth, pressing hard enough to pinch his upper lip against his teeth. He hoped she wouldn't bite him up too much, right before they were supposed to go home.

She twisted and pushed him over, lay heavily on top of him, moved her hips and shoulders. She kissed him hard. She said, "I don't fuck retards," and slid down his bathing trunks. She arranged her long hippy skirt over them like a tent and stared into his eyes with theatrical intensity. Afterwards, she cried again. She said, "I'm so worried you'll forget me when I go to school." He kissed her tears and muttered against her neck. They kissed, crying, and he made love to her again, until the sandy soil rubbed his knees raw and they moved inside, where they took a long shower, after which he rubbed her all over with hemp body lotion from Bed Bath, and Beyond and they did sixty-nine on the long oak table. They fell asleep on the musty king-sized bed in the master bedroom.

They made love again in the morning, lazy and groggy and lingering over each other, then showered and closed up the house. Jack told Meaghan they didn't have to clean the place too well, because his brother Randall was coming up the following weekend. From the porch where she was shaking out a rug, she said, "Oh – fuck him!" Randall didn't like any of Jack's friends.

They stopped at a little breakfast joint on the way home. The walls were littered with plastic strawberries and fake flowers, and they held hands and smoked cigarettes at the table. The waitress was wrinkled and bent, but wore a crisp pink diner waitress uniform. Meaghan nicknamed her Eunice, and made up a story about what she was like when she was a kid. Meaghan said Eunice was a hellraiser, going out with a different boy every night, French kissing on the first date, parking in old cars like the ones sometimes displayed outside of the Jukebox Diner at the shopping center.

Jack frowned and said, "Ugh."

She looked at him seriously, took his hands in hers. "You better want to fuck me when I'm old and wrinkled." She scrunched up her sunburned nose and he leaned across the table, kissed her and mumbled, "Give me some time to work up to it." She giggled and pushed him away as the waitress put a plate of hotcakes smothered in strawberries and whipped cream between them.

He talked to her on the phone only once the first week she was away at school, and she mostly said I miss you, and talked dirty. She said orientation was lame, but that there were some goth girls on her floor she liked, that they had seriously pissed off this one Barbie doll on her hall, though she didn't say how. She told him she had a secret crush on one of the goth girls, but that he didn't have to worry. She said "I love you," and waited for him to say it, and then said "all mine" before she hung up.

Jack sat in Mr. Kressler's class, copying notes from the board for their Friday quiz, or in avionics lab, playing Flight Simulator on an old PC, thinking only of Meaghan. He got himself sprung from algebra 2 and English so he could shoot video for the yearbook, and he found himself intruding on his own classes to make the film.

In homeroom one Wednesday, he got another note from his guidance counselor, Mr. Sikorski, who, Jack was sure, wanted to talk to him about his future. Everyone blew Mr. Sikorski off, even the rich kids and the brains. Jack was sure the tall bald man would laugh at him if he told him he thought about his future with Meaghan, a house, and yard, and kids. He knew Mr. Sikorski wasn't interested in helping him get to that place. Jack kept the appointment anyway and showed up outside of his office door at third period.

The office was small but sunny, decorated with pictures of college athletics and pennants from Penn State, Pitt, Slippery Rock, and LaRoche. A maroon CMU pennant hung in the corner above the aluminum-framed window. The guidance counselor said, "You aren't Jack Grappa, are you?"

Jack said, "That's me," as brightly as he could.

Mr. Sikorski adjusted his glasses and opened Jack's file. "We haven't had a chance to talk before." He flipped through green grade sheets and pink progress reports. "This says you're a whiz with film and video." He looked at Jack, who sat on his hands and nodded.

"But your other grades are . . . well, you seem to . . . you're a little inconsistent."

"I know," he said.

He looked at Jack over the file and said, "Where do you see yourself next year?"

Jack looked at the floor and said, "I was kind of hoping we could talk about that."

"Well, are you thinking about college?"

"No. I'm not that smart, not that way," he said.

"Trust me, Jack, your grades aren't that bad. You aren't going to get into Carnegie Mellon, but you can probably get into IUP or U. Pitt Titusville?"

Jack brightened at the thought—what if he could go to college with Meaghan the next year? Would they let them room together? But even as the thoughts formed, he knew he couldn't do it. She was smart, and it was a lot of work for her. He imagined papers and tests and presentations piling up, imagined wasting his parents' money, imagined their disappointed faces.

He and Mr. Sikorski made an action plan together, and the older man got genuinely excited. They decided he would go to every English class and get special tutoring from academic services. They decided to have him tested for ADD and to test to see if his weak eye was affecting his reading. Mr. Sikorski said they could get him "accommodations," which Jack understood to be more trips to the SPED shed, and he knew he'd rather be caught dead than be seen going in and out of the white aluminum trailer permanently parked by the athletic field door.

Jack wondered if the tall man knew he had never read a whole book. He read six trade magazines a month in the studio, on everything from home video to sound engineering, and Dr. Deeb, the principal, would smile at him in the hall and say, "What are we going to do around here when you're gone, Mr. Grappa?" He knew the name of every piece of equipment he'd never get to lay his hands on. Everyone knew there weren't any studio engineering jobs for Oc Ed kids; everyone knew Oc Ed was a way to keep kids like him from just beating the joke to the punch line and dropping out and getting a full time job at the mall.

He knew Mr. Sikorski was right—he needed a college degree to do anything that didn't totally suck, and Jack was miserable at the idea of having to stay in school a minute longer than he had to. The bell rang and he excused himself, shook the counselor's hand, and took a sheaf of application instructions and a handout on writing application essays. He also grabbed one on writing a resume, though he didn't know why you needed one if you didn't have anything to put on it.

He went into English class at fourth period, and took his seat in the third row. The teacher handed out copies of a book called Fahrenheit 451, and talked about it being a science fiction novel, which got his attention. He wondered if he could maybe do this—English was his worst class, and the one he avoided most often. He carried a C most of the time because Ms. D'Urso would tell them the stories in class, and he remembered enough to get by. He could read the words, but he couldn't follow stories or imagine people. He wondered why they couldn't just watch movies and talk about that.

He went to history and wrote the notes Mr. Hanks wrote on the board. Every day Mr. Hanks wrote notes on the board, except Fridays, when he gave a quiz on the week's notes. It was Jack's best class, even though a year later he wouldn't remember what eras the class had studied. During his free period he tried to read Fahrenheit 451 for about twenty minutes before he gave up and decided to see if Blockbuster had a movie version.

The last two weeks in September went by and he didn't hear from Meaghan. At first, he was annoyed, and he flirted with Leslie Donovan a little in their business fundamentals class, and with Damhnait Monaghan in homeroom. Her name was pronounced dav-net, but he called her "Dammit Monongahela," and she smiled at him and her eyes were bright green. He thought about the sophomore girls who passed him in the hall and knew his name, even though he didn't know theirs. But he couldn't seriously entertain the idea of being with anyone but Meaghan; she was his best friend, and the thought of betraying her, even in little ways, nagged at him. In the AV room, he watched footage he'd shot of her before she had asked him out eighteen months earlier, noticed how his camera moved over her face and body like his hands eventually would.

By the end of the second week he was frantic. He made up reasons why she might not call: long distance charges, her schoolwork, her busy social life. One Friday, in health, they watched a movie in which a girl Meaghan's age drank a lot at a fraternity party. Guys in sweaters poured drinks for her, and then the room started to spin; Jack was disgusted by the amateurish camera work, thinking that he didn't even need a dolly to shoot a better panorama than this.

The camera zoomed in as the fraternity brothers gathered around the girl's unconscious form, and when one touched her chest, several boys in the class guffawed and one made a snorting, honking noise. Jack felt a wash of anger and panic. He turned around and glared at them. The movie ended with the fraternity brothers being arrested, and with shadowy footage of the girl being escorted to an ambulance, horror in her eyes. The announcer said, "One in three women will be sexually assaulted while she is in college. Will alcohol make you a victim?" The announcer paused for a few beats. "Will it make you a criminal?"

Before the credits stopped rolling, Coach Mick switched off the projector. Looking at the boys in the back of the room, he shouted, "How in the hell is that funny?" which set them off again.

Jack didn't know their names—one of the kids was Miller, but he didn't know if it was his first or last name. He'd found it funny when they had cheered every time marijuana was mentioned during the Drug Abuse Resistance Education movie, or when they sang the Trojan Man theme song every time condoms were mentioned during the AIDS film, but this felt different. He turned in his seat to glare at them again. He noticed that the girls in the room were mostly looking at the ground or their feet, and that made him angry. Worse, he felt like he was being judged, like he should get up and throw a desk at them or something to prove he wasn't like them. Coach Mick said, "Well, what's so goddamned funny?" They giggled, tittered, and one did a fairly convincing impression of an elephant's trumpet. And then the bell rang, and they skittered out the back door of the classroom under the coach's red-faced glower.

Jack worried that Meaghan had gotten drunk and been taken advantage of, worried that she'd turn her blame inwards and that it was already driving a wedge between them. He vowed he'd love her no matter what. He vowed he'd kill the bastard who hurt a hair on her head. He watched tape he'd shot of her the year before, her face on half a dozen Sony monitors at once, and he worried.

She answered on the first ring late on Sunday night, and he said hello. She squealed his name and said, "I'm sorry I didn't call. It's been something else up here." She sounded out of breath, like she'd been running, and he was so relieved that pure joy stopped his throat. He thought about her body after she went out jogging, about beads of perspiration on her heaving belly, about her damp sports bra hanging over his bedstead.

"Are you okay," he asked, with tears in his eyes.

"I'm great, Jack!" He sniffled and coughed to cover the fact that he was all choked up. She hesitated and said, "I'm Isabella!"

"What?"

"Isabella, from Measure for Measure. It's a play. I'm in a Shakespeare play. I'm working my ass off," she said.

"Oh," he said, grinning. "What's it about?"

"I play the chaste virgin everyone wants to fuck," she said, and he could feel her sexy crooked smile through the phone.

"I wish you were here," he said.

"I wish you were here," she said. "I wish you could see this place, I mean, experience it. We work and work and work and then get totally shitfaced in the woods, and the cops come, but they're only campus cops, and you don't get kicked out unless you do something really stupid or violent. And it's just kids, everywhere. And now I'm Isabella."

He thought again about the possibility that he could get in to IUP. "I could ask my mom. I could probably come up next weekend." He added, "Check the place out for myself."

"That would be fantastic, Jack. Holy shit! I have anthro. I'll call you."

Jack found his mother smoking at the kitchen table, sat down and shook a Marlboro from her pack. She reached over and lit it and said, "How's it going, Jacko," in a way that made it seem she already knew.

He said, "Ma, I think I want to go visit Meaghan up in Indiana this weekend."

She told him his father needed him to finish his brother's garage. "Somebody has to stay sober to drive Randall to the hospital," she said, rasping her hard-smoked laugh. "Can you go next weekend?" she asked, and he couldn't say no.

Jack and his dad drove the four miles to Randall's on Saturday morning. Jack was quiet and unfocused, drinking coffee, smoking, and waiting for his thoughts to stop racing. Jack's dad was popping Tums and Tylenols, holding a cigarette but rarely drawing on it. As they pulled in to the drive in front of Randall and Lisa's beige split-level, he said, "Jackalope, what do you think your big brother has planned for us today?"

Jack replied, "I'll bet he starts yelling at you first. I'm staying out of his way."

"It's a bet," his father said.

Randall came out, his face still red and completely hairless from the explosion that had burned his garage to the ground. He didn't look at Jack, but said, "I got the demo done yesterday, and the materials are out back. Let's get to work."

Jack snapped off measurements with a metal tape and thick pencil, cutting two-by-sixes with the miter saw and running them to the two older men who worked in silence. His brother popped can after can of Iron City Light, and his dad drank from a big jar of ice and Coke that Jack knew was spiked with George Dickel bourbon. Jack thought about Meaghan as he worked, let his mind drift to their time at the lake, and to playing pool with her in his parents' rec room, and he played her promises over in his mind. Instead of making it easier, he felt a taint of anxiety clinging to every memory. Jack knew that later, as their arms and backs got sore, his dad wouldn't care if he hit the jar a little, too.

At noon, Jack's dad let out a loud, low whistle and called "lunch!" Jack couldn't look at his brother's poached face or the fine stubble clinging in patches to his head. Randall whined, "Come on! Let's get this done!"

The elder Grappa ignored him, and walked towards the house, dropping his hammer and pulling up his pants as he made his way towards the sliding patio doors. Randall's wife, Lisa, was putting sandwiches together at the kitchen counter, both kids strapped to their chairs and munching away quietly. She gave the men ham and cheese, and they drank tumblers full of Kool-Aid.

They had the frame done by three o'clock, and the roof laid out in big triangles on the lawn. Randall was getting tired, and Jack watched as he balanced on the top step of a rickety stepladder, swinging a framing hammer, doing a dance every three or four falls to try to keep on his perch. Jack kept trying to catch his father's eye, knowing he could crack his old man up, and that Randall would go apeshit if they started laughing at him. The two of them were on the verge of giggling like little kids as Randall finally slipped, recovered his balance, slid to the concrete pad, and just missed hitting himself in the head with his own hammer. Jack and his father looked down at their work, trying not to laugh as Randall kicked the ladder to pieces, swearing and muttering and rubbing a new bruise on his tortured scalp.

They knocked off at seven, the sun turning the sky brilliant orange and yellow. Randall was still hammering away at sheathing, scowling at them for quitting before dark. Jack's dad said, "We framed 280 square feet and a roof – I think we can leave the rest until tomorrow," meaning he was going home before Randall flipped out, and Jack should come with him. They said goodbye to the kids and Lisa, drove home, watched The Terminator on HBO, drank George Dickel, and smoked cigarettes. Jack's mom made chip-chop ham sandwiches, and they ate ring bologna and cheese, and finished with big bowls of chocolate chip ice cream and Manhattans. Jack was shit-faced by eleven, and dreamed about Meaghan falling off of a ladder into his arms, felt he was falling, woke up, went to the bathroom, and vomited. He brushed his teeth and went back to sleep immediately, his head pounding and his stomach empty with longing.

Sunday, father and son woke hungry, ate lunch-meat omelets at the kitchen counter, and got to Randall's early, driving the ridge above fields where the corn was already turning brown, through woods spotted with yellow and red. Randall greeted them in the driveway, and Jack resisted the urge to look away from his brother's face, his red eyes and red skull. The ground was slippery with dew, and the garage was already sheathed in plywood.

They worked steadily, Jack and his father cutting pieces of roofing plywood and passing them up to Randall, who nailed them down with a pneumatic nailer. The thunk, thunk, thunk of the nailer beat a tattoo into the chill air, punctuated by Jack's brother cursing at corners that shifted, nails that missed joists, or at the perpetual discomfort of his widespread first- and second-degree burns. Jack thought about what her life might be like, the things that were keeping her so preoccupied. He'd seen Animal House and Revenge of the Nerds, but they didn't really help— he figured there was partying, but he couldn't imagine what her classes were like. He thought of the comedian Sam Kinison playing a history teacher opposite Rodney Dangerfield in Back to School. Kinison screamed something about the Vietnam War, and Jack thought about how he really didn't understand the scene because he didn't know anything about Vietnam. He wondered why he found it funny anyway.

They laid sheets of half-inch in place and Randall moved the nailer fast, thunk, thunk, thunk, thunk, shoving Jack out of the way if he wasn't quick enough. They laid the last sheet of plywood in place, and Randall almost knocked Jack off the roof as he moved the nailer, thunk, thunk, thunk, until he drove a nail between his thumb and forefinger. He tore the skin loose from the plywood, and teetered on the edge, shouting obscenities. Jack slid down the ladder and hooted, but his father glared at him, and he stopped. The elder Grappa asked Randall if he wanted to go to the ER. Randall climbed down, dripping blood on the roof and smearing it on the ladder, and stomped inside. He came back with paper towels wadded around his hand, wrapping it with duct tape, his gray sweatshirt and old jeans stained brown and red. Neither Jack nor his father said a word. Jack and Randall worked on underlayment, stapling thick tarpaper to the roof in long sheets. They stopped at noon for sandwiches that Lisa brought out on a plastic Star Wars Episode 1 tray, and Jack cracked one of Randall's beers.

Randall looked at Jack, sneered, and said, "I should call the cops, you little shit."

Jack shot him the bird and took a long pull at the can. Randall smacked it into his face, showering both of them with beer, and they would have come to blows except that when Randall made a fist the pain bent him over, and the elder Grappa ordered them to settle down in his old-bear gravel voice: "Randall, your brother just built you a goddamned garage, you won't let him have a beer?"

Randall swiped at the beer can again, but Jack backed up and out of his reach, making a show of finishing every drop. Randall glared; "My house, my rules," he said, and stormed back to the worksite.

Randall disconnected the framing nailer and snapped a roofing nailer to the coupling at the end of his air hose. He rammed a coil of short, broad-headed nails into the canister and threaded them through the mechanism, cocked it like some kind of sci-fi weapon, and yelled, "Well, where are my shingles?"

Jack's father cleared his throat, and the air compressor stopped its rattle and hum as if obeying him. He said, "Why don't you let your brother work up on the roof, and you come down and run shingles to me?"

Randall turned and glared at Jack, then climbed the ladder and hopped onto the slope of the roof. "Because he won't fuck up carrying shingles." He gestured at the roof, the nail gun in his left hand, his finger brushing the trigger. "I don't want to have to redo a leaky roof because this lazy shit."

"Fuck you, Randall," Jack said, and he'd have punched his brother if he hadn't been standing on the ground below him.

"Oh, fuck me? Nice. My own house. In front of your father. Real nice." He threw his arms out to the sides and yelled, "I know you have your head stuck up your ass, and all you care about is your slut, but you better…" As he spoke Randall's arm came down, the nailer's press-in safety tip grazed his leg, and the machine spat two nails into Randall's kneecap halfway through the word "disappointment."

Randall screamed, and Jack made it up the ladder in time to keep him from falling off the roof. Randall glared at him as Jack eased him down the ladder, helping him favor his left leg. Randall was weeping when his brother wheeled him into the ER, and he passed out from the pain of having duct tape removed from his mangled and swollen hand. Jack and his father worked the rest of the evening finishing Randall's roof, and Jack played with his niece and nephew while Lisa went to pick up Randall and bring him home.

Jack only got to talk to Meaghan once in the next few weeks, and he tried to fill the minutes and hours. He went to several job fairs after school. Mr. Amicci gave him a pass to leave school for a day, and he drove to Oakdale, Bridgeville, and then all the way to Cranberry. At the last one, he stood in front of the Navy recruiting table for a long time, looking at pictures of kids his age working on indecipherable electronics panels. A guy in his twenties, flat-topped and uniformed, caught Jack's eye and said, "You want to sit down and rap about your future, buddy?" He flashed a smile and crossed his well-muscled forearms over his chest. Jack imagined the scene in Full Metal Jacket where they beat the fat man until he is a psychotic killing machine. He mumbled no and ducked into the crowd. He'd shrugged off AMWAY and Herbalife shills because his brother had been involved with both, and he knew they were ripoffs.

He thought about his friends: Meaghan, who wanted to be an actress, Jeremy Buckman who was already taking physics classes on the internet, who got mailers from famous colleges like Johns Hopkins and MIT. He realized he didn't know where either school was. He thought about Abbi, who had started going to her mother's church every Sunday in hopes of scoring a congregation scholarship, who was always talking about developing the community service part of her application, who wanted to be an archeologist. He imagined her, short, with her boyish haircut and smartass comments, running from Amazons and stealing magical treasure from Nazis, swinging across a chasm on her bullwhip, and he realized he didn't even know what archeology really was.

He walked up to the PennTech Career Training Academy table. He'd seen the commercials on daytime TV: "Be an Avionics Technician! Diesel Repair is a guaranteed future!" A too-thin old man in a very old suit called out, "What do you think young fella? You good with machines?" Jack took some brochures, imagined himself stuck with a bunch of motorheads stripping down engines, barking knuckles, growing farther away from Meaghan and her dorm room. Anthro, he thought. What the fuck is anthro?

He went to the Electrician's Union table, but it was all more school, or being yelled at by dicks like Randall, or both. Finally, he took a bunch of brochures from the Community College of Allegheny County. School. He had to go to school. The rest was fast food and retail, missing fingers and cancer. He took applications for a jewelry sales position, and for a men's clothing store, but he didn't fill anything out.

Jack had been sitting with Abbi Macdonald and Jeremy Buckman at lunch for nine years. Alberto Munno was an old friend of Jack's father and grandfather, and the old man had been like another grandfather to Jack. When he died the kids were in the tenth grade. Jack walked around in a fog for months. Jack started telling Abbi and Jeremy Munno's stories, and started making up new ones.

It hurt to remember the old man, but Jack felt close to him when he told the stories. He told them about Munno getting drunk and totaling a rental car by driving it into the side of his own above-ground swimming pool. He told them about Munno throwing a Native American spear he'd bought on eBay through the window of a North Fayette police car, "piss drunk and howling about how he was a warrior chieftain," something he'd been watching on The History Channel. He told them about Munno getting the FBI and the ATF called out to his place because he used some quarter sticks to blow up a couple of propane tanks at the exact moment a C130 from the Airforce base was passing overhead. He told them Munno was dead, but he'd never been caught. The last story made Pepsi come out of Jeremy's nose.

Before Jack knew it, it was late October, and though he was as devoted to Meaghan as ever, he grew less hurt by her relative silence. He was busy, he thought, and so was she. But he burned to see her, and when he got her on the phone a week before Halloween, he said, "Fuck it. I'm coming to see you. I miss you so much."

She was quiet for a minute, and she said she missed him, too, and they were having a party, and he should bring a costume and his drinking shoes, because if he didn't dress up, he'd have to go naked—it was a rule, and, she said, there would probably be naked people there. She said "It's going to be so good to see you," pausing between words for emphasis. The raw current of his beautiful Meaghan coursed through him again, and he failed his history quiz, even though he had copied the notes from the board. He was going to see her, to hold her pale naked body to his lips and drink her in.

Between rock blocks the radio in Jack's truck said Western Pennsylvania was due for some nasty, cold fall rain, and Accuweather called for early ice storms between Lake Erie and I-80. He thought of his cousins in Warren, how they sometimes had flurries in July and August, how Titusville could have snow days in mid September. He watched the last light play on nicotine clouds as he sat listening to Dr. Altenderfer drone in life sciences. He saw the pounding rain, the low clouds and blowing sheets of water, thought of Meaghan's hair, wet in a summer storm, with the rain streaming down her body as she had posed on a glacial rock and teased him by lifting her skirt and running her fingers up her thigh, and he resolved himself: fuck it.

He spun his tires on the gravel of the student lot, driving his truck hard, passing cars on the straightaway near the new development, kicking up rooster tails of water where silt had closed the storm drains. He would be under her, over her, his mouth full of her—in her dorm room, with all of the pornographic possibilities attached to the phrase. He would be in her arms, and the creeping dread of having to face sudden and inevitable manhood would dissolve for a while. He hoped someone would have liquor, because beer made him have to burp and pee.

The first flakes vaporized against his windshield as he merged onto 79 north, following signs for Titusville and Erie. Meagan was less than two hundred miles away, and he had to fight to keep his speed within reason as the trees and scrub collected snow. He hit the brakes just in time, a state trooper angled behind a billboard that read "Slow Down. The Life You Save May Be Your Own," poised to fuck up his weekend.

It was dark by 4 p.m., and snow was falling thick and heavy

one minute, and the next, rain was making icicles on his radio antenna and windshield wiper blades. He tried to keep his speed up, but kept inching down as he passed stranded cars and trucks, as he felt the back wheels under the empty bed try to kick loose. He was relieved when he finally got to his exit, creeping along the highway at thirty miles per hour, Meagan seeming to grow farther away.

The off-ramp was banked and curved, and as soon as it flattened out at the bottom the little pickup went into a skid. He fought it, knowing he shouldn't, and the truck spun slowly around before the tires found a bare patch of asphalt and it lurched to a stop facing the wrong direction on a two-lane road that had been a modern highway sixty years before. Jack braced himself for the crunch of metal on metal, but no one was around; no one had even seen him spin out.

He eased the truck to the top of the first rise, and fought his impulse to hit the brakes as he coasted down the other side. He quickly found that he would have to keep up his momentum to make it to the top of each rise, as his tires spun before he gained the peak of each hill. Long descents were the worst, and he felt roller-coaster sick each time he touched the brakes or took a turn. He watched the odometer; it took him forty-five minutes to travel eight miles.

He stopped at a crest overlooking a deep valley, and couldn't keep going for the dread he felt. His headlights shone yellow and weak through the rime of ice that covered his truck. His head ached; he had a lazy eye and poor depth perception, and the strain of looking past snowflakes and raindrops into the white-and-black tunnel of frozen trees and iced-over asphalt weakened the muscle so that he saw double. WDVE crackled and became faint. He thought about stopping, pulling over, sleeping, waiting for the plow trucks to come, but realized how dangerous it would be to sit with his lights off on the narrow berm, how a truck might come along and hit him, how a statey might come along and send him back to the highway and home.

He put a Dave Matthews CD in his CD player. The valley was shallow, but the road curved slightly, and Jack spun out halfway down the hill, the truck revolving once and then twice, gravity pulling it down and around as Jack recognized g-forces, thought about the guy with the apple tree, and about Einstein's ideas, which he understood from watching The Next Generation. He turned in the direction of the skid and righted himself, hooting like one of the Dukes of Hazard as he found himself barreling down once more, accelerating into the curve a little. He imagined that the wet, heavy flakes were neutrinos and laser beams bouncing off of his shields, that he was carrying the cure to a plague to a beleaguered colony on the edge of space, that he was escaping a prison deep within some alien world of ice and rain.

He got stuck on the next rise as the road took a hard left and he had no choice but to brake, and he sat cursing the road and his truck and the Pennsylvania countryside, the rain and the ice and his stupid bad timing. He thumped the dash and punched the steering wheel and felt like crying. Finally he pushed down easy on the accelerator and started creeping forward on a relatively level stretch. He gained a little momentum, but as he climbed he felt the truck slipping, then the tires spun, and he was sliding backwards with the accelerator floored.

He stopped, sobbing with anger, and then slowly turned the truck around. He floored it down the hill, not caring anymore, and when he ran out of momentum going up the other side, he backed up into the silvered brush at the edge of the road and half-slid into position facing downhill again. Then he plowed ahead, careening through the turn where he'd panicked before, and nearly gained the next crest. It took him two more tries to beat the mile-long incline, and he was wet and sour with sweat when he lit a victory cigarette.

The next downhill was easier, if no less terrifying, and he found himself in a dark, deserted little town. The road curved past a cement plant and an abandoned AGWAY, and streetlights played on the thick crust of ice that covered everything. He had never been so tired. He imagined telling her about it, his ordeal, his death-defying scramble to hold her in his arms, and imagined her saying "My hero," with only a trace of irony.

He could scarcely believe it when the road leveled out under streetlights and he saw an enormous green BP sign. He pulled in the lot, and battled the wind to the door. He pushed the door closed behind him, and squinted into the fluorescent glare. The old man behind the counter said, "You got ten minutes! The plow's coming through in fifteen and I'm going home behind it, whether the sonofabitch I work for says I can or not!" Jack went to the men's room, then poured himself a big Styrofoam cup of milky coffee, decided to grab a couple of hot dogs and a pack of peanut M&Ms. He asked for Marlboro Reds and paid the old man, who followed him out to lock up the store.

He put his food and coffee in his cab and helped the man pull a tarp off of the front half of his old Impala, ice packed into the crevices and gluing it to the car in places. He went to start the car, and Jack heard the unmistakable whump of a dead battery. Cursing, the old man got out and asked Jack for a jump. He got cables from the trunk of his car, and they banged Jack's hood until it groaned open. Jack sat in his cab, gunning his engine, until the man's car started spitting smoke. The man slammed Jack's hood and threw the jumper cables into the Impala's passenger seat, and held up one finger for Jack to wait. He sat shaking ice out of his hair and eating his hot dogs, blasting the heater. He watched the giant snow plow sail through the blizzard, marveled at the arc of its spume. The old man came back with packages under his arms and bottles in each hand, bow-armed and bow-legged. He stopped and pulled each of Jack's wiper blades free and threw them into the snow behind him, and expertly attached new wipers to each of the arms. Then he filled Jack's reservoir, and set several jugs in the back of the truck. He hollered, "It's on the asshole I work for," and disappeared into his car. Jack followed him out, spraying his windshield with blue solvent and watching the Impala's tail lights, and they caught up to the plow, cinders and kernels of salt clinking against the floor pan of the truck.

It was slow going, and the yellow strobes on the plow made his eye drift even more, but he made it to the entrance to the campus where men in Bobcats and John Deere earthmovers dumped slush and snow in the drainage ditches. He got directions from a man wearing a rabbit fur hat, and pulled up to her dorm. It was nearly midnight, and he was wet and exhausted.

He went up to the little glass enclosure that sheltered the entrance to the door and keyed her room number into the intercom. It rang a dozen times and then hung up. He tried again, and then a third time, but got no response. He went back to the truck and sat in the cab, wondering what to do. He wasn't sure he was supposed to be there, and he didn't want to have to explain himself to a cop. He let the engine run to warm up, and then shut it off and did his best to stretch out on the bench seat, a wadded-up tee shirt under his head and an old sweatshirt for a blanket.

He woke up to a light shining through the crust of ice inside the windows of the cab, and was so cold his fingers and toes hurt. He tried to roll down his window and couldn't, unlocked his door, and threw his weight against it to open it.

A policeman wearing the college's crest on his orange slicker said, "Are you okay? It's too cold to be out here. Are you locked out?"

Jack shivered so much he had a hard time getting the words "girlfriend" and "visiting" and "not answering" out, and the policeman checked his ID, took his bag and helped him into the building. The cop said, "Now, Jonathan, I just want to help you out, keep you safe. You don't look too bad, but I want you to get a shower and get someplace warm for a while, maybe have some soup or something. Who are you visiting?" Jack sat down on an orange couch with wooden armrests and said "Meaghan Holt." His head felt heavy and he ached all over, and his skin burned in the warmer air. The cop spoke into his radio, "Dispatch, this is one-one-six. Can we try to find a Meaghan Holt? She has a visitor who's been sleeping in his truck, white male, five-six, one hundred sixty, maybe sixteen years old." He brought Jack a woolen army blanket, and Jack huddled under it and shivered.

Jack was asleep when Meaghan came through the door to the lobby. He came to hearing her voice, and made out that she was talking to the cop whose name he couldn't remember. He sat up and the room seemed to wobble before it settled. Opening his eyes hurt, and moving his legs so that he could sit up hurt even worse. His throat was swollen and his nose plugged. And he still felt cold. The cop left, and then he was in her arms, her hair so warm against his cheek that he could feel her smell through his skin. "I need to sleep," he said. "Let's go to your room and get some juice and spend all day in bed." He hoped she would do most of the work, but was already feeling his want and lack.

She guided him up some stairs and used a key at the end of a bright green nylon strap to unlock a heavy wooden door. Her room was divided down the middle with a line of masking tape. Meaghan's side was obvious: black comforter and red sheets, books about vampires and Wicca on the shelves, a clock radio that looked like a human skull, a poster of Jim Morrison looking like he was being crucified. Her roommate wasn't there. Her comforter had rainbow-colored teddy bears on it, and she had a poster of Jesus on the cross above the bed. Meaghan left quickly as he started to take off his clothing, and he climbed into her bed and fell asleep waiting for her.

When he woke, Meaghan was looking out the window, wearing only a thong and a Bride of Frankenstein wig. A techno beat came from the tinny speakers of her clock radio, and she danced as she zipped up the front of her black vinyl corset. She noticed him and said, "Good morning, sunshine!" before stepping into a pair of lace-trimmed granny panties.

He ached all over and was so thirsty he thought he might cry.

"You better get your costume on, Jackanapes," she said. "People are going to be here any minute."

Jack got up and looked in the mini fridge. He found a can of diet Coke and took it out.

"Oh, don't drink that," she said. She crinkled up her nose. "That's my roommate's." She gestured to the poster of Jesus on the cross behind her. "We do not get along."

Jack went into the hall to get a drink from the water fountain, but someone had covered the spout with a condom. He felt dizzy and hungry as he walked down to the lobby and scooped water from the faucet in the men's room. Then he felt nauseous, and leaned his head against the cool metal of the paper towel dispenser.

When he dragged himself upstairs again and opened the door to Meaghan's room, a puffy-faced redhead with bangs cut so short they stuck out like quills looked at him, smiled, and shouted "Shut the DOOR!" Five guys guys a little older than him, all wearing Pirates caps and jerseys glared at him from under the brims of their hats.

"Jackanapes!" Meaghan hollered, sitting on the bed, the silk of her drawers bunching up. She leaned over and poured him a cup of Hawaiian punch, and he drank it quickly, shivering in his sweaty t-shirt. He knew she was introducing people but couldn't quite hear everything she was saying. She lit a cigarette and handed it to him, but he waved it away. Meaghan whooped and stood up; he thought how good she looked, how completely perfect, even under her ghoulish white makeup. One of the boys handed him a full plastic cup; he took it and tasted alcohol, but it didn't seem like much, and anyway it burned away his raw swollen throat.

He woke in Meaghan's bed, turned on his side, red vomit caked on his shirt, the pillow and the comforter. His head hurt a little, and he felt both nauseous and hungry. He carried his bag down the silent hallway, and looked for a door marked Men, remembering that there wasn't one. He knocked softly at the door marked Women, and pushed the door open gingerly. When the fluorescent lights flickered on automatically he jumped back, gasping, and then laughed at himself.

He stripped off his soiled clothing in the shower stall, washed the vomit off of his face and out of his hair, gargled with the warm water, cautiously swallowed mouthfuls. He wrung out his t-shirt and pyjama pants and dressed in his Halloween costume, black pants and a thin black sweater (he had planned to go as Neo from The Matrix). As he was pushing his wet clothing back into his backpack, he heard the door open and he froze: he felt the shame of discovery, imagined being arrested, the campus cops no longer friendly, imagined himself on the Sex Offenders registry, hate mail stuffed in his parents' mailbox. He heard the sound of a girl vomiting and sobbing softly, and made his escape.

The door to Meaghan's room was ajar, and the lights were on. He thought she was there to look in on him, to make sense of the whole weekend. He turned the corner and stopped.

Meaghan's roommate was a tall girl with an overbite and braces, wan blond hair she wore cut to her shoulders, with bangs. She was dressed in a fuzzy white sweater and a long denim skirt. A small gold cross glittered over the sharp lines her bra cut under her sweater. She looked at him, scowled, and said, "Who the fuck are you?"

He mumbled, "Meaghan's friend. From back home."

"Well where the fuck is she? Look at this place!"

He looked around. The room reeked of cherry vomit and cigarettes. There was a pool of punch drying on the floor and another of beer seeping under the closet door. The floor was muddy with footprints and cigarette ash. She turned and stepped a few feet closer to her bed. "Jesus Christ!" she yelled, stamping her foot. She pointed to a sticky mass in the center of her Care Bears comforter. "Fucking perfect," she said through clenched teeth. She turned to look at Jack.

"Are you Jack? Jack? Meaghan's supposed boyfriend?" He nodded. "She talked about you when we first got here, before I hated her fucking guts." She looked at him and her expression softened a little. Then she gritted her teeth. "You're probably an okay guy. If you haven't figured it out, Meaghan is a whore. A dirty filthy slut. She has sex with different guys in here all the time, sometimes while I'm here, trying to sleep. She was fucking a campus cop in here one time. She's done like half the baseball team, and our baseball team sucks."

He stood looking at her, waiting for the punch line. She walked over to him and gave him a stiff, polite pat on the shoulder. "I know it's hard to hear that," she said. "Find a decent person. She said what a great guy you are. Find someone who deserves you." She pulled her hand back and said, "Now clean this fucking place up."

He looked around, making sure he hadn't forgotten anything, turned towards the door and flipped her off over his shoulder. "Oh, perfect," she yelled after him. "I hope you and your skank both get AIDS!"

At the bottom of the stairs he heard angry whispers, and recognized the remains of Meaghan's hairdo. She was wearing a grey Pirates jersey and basketball shorts that were way too big for her. She was talking to one of the baseball cap boys, who was still wearing his cap pulled down over his eyes. He glared at Jack and stiffened. Jack looked at him, shook his head, and looked at her. Rumpled and hungover, she still glittered in the weak yellow light coming through the frosted windows. "I'm going home," he said. "If you even care, I'm leaving."

"Of course I care," she said. "Why would you say that?"

Jack looked at her, his face registering just a little bit of disgust and anger under his limp cheek muscles. "I'm not stupid. Not THAT stupid, anyway."

"Oh, Jack," she said, making a show of reaching out for his hand. "You're jealous. I'm sorry. I knew this would be too much for you to handle, but . . . you know, I didn't know how to say no when you asked. I, well, I knew it was a bad idea for you to come up this weekend."

He looked at her face to see if she was laughing at him, but she had a frozen look of pity, a thin, knowing smile, pasted on. He said, "Whatever," and pushed past her to the door. The baseball cap boy yelled "Go fuck yourself" after him, and he heard them arguing as he threw his bag into his truck, fired it up, backed out of his space and spun tire out of the lot.

He stopped at a McDonald's and ate 99-cent double cheeseburgers, one after another, and calmed his roiling stomach with a strawberry shake. He went to the men's room, bought some coffee to go, and drove away from the melting ice into a warm autumn day.

Jack's parents had been worried, and they both held him in hugs for a long time. His dad grounded him, but they didn't yell. He spent most of the next week in his room, first recovering, then playing sick and surfing the web for porn and watching bad action movies on cable. The porn didn't work; every time he got excited and closed his eyes, he saw her giving another guy a blowjob, her being fucked by baseball players, his time with her, her promises and his own.

His mom gave him worried looks and felt his forehead; his dad was more quiet than usual. Once he sat down on the edge of Jack's bed and looked at his shoes. He sipped from his glass and said, "War is hell, Jacko," and sat there for a while before he patted Jack's leg and went out to the kitchen.

He went back to school and started work on the video yearbook, wishing he could do something like it for the rest of his life—set the markers, grab the video from the master, line everything up, and drop the clip. He watched his classmates ham for the camera dressed in their athletic uniforms, their street clothes, and their homecoming suits and dresses. He watched the Fayette Ram do somersaults down the sidelines, watched girls he didn't even know blow kisses to his lens. He dodged questions, and thought about killing himself.

A week before Thanksgiving, Abbi drove her Ranger onto his parents' lawn and knocked on their door. He could hear her talking to his mom, telling her they had plans, that he was so forgetful. She threw open his door and said, "Get your shit together, Grappa!"

He squinted at her and shook a cigarette out of a crushed package. "What?"

"You're coming with me," she said.

"Where?"

"Fuck if I know. We need to talk." She led him by the hand through the living room, sharing a knowing look with his mom, who chuckled. Outside, she turned to face him and said, "What did that bitch do to you?"

"Nothing," he said, but the sound didn't come out.

She poked him hard in the stomach. "Spill it!"

"Not here," he said, and walked to her truck. They rode along the ridge between Bridgeville and Oakdale, hugging the treacherous switchbacks of the old road, and Jack told her about that weekend—the drive, the cop, the boys in baseball caps, the roommate. He added, "I don't know what to think. I mean, what if her roommate is just a bitch, causing trouble. I don't want to be, like, jealous or possessive or whatever." He remembered the terms from a health class video called, "Responsible Relationships."

"Jesus, Jack," Abbi said, sliding onto a gravel pulloff. She turned in her seat so that she could look him in the eye, and his heart tried to beat out her words. "She's a fucking slut, dude. I'm sorry, but she's a slut. I never liked her. She's a total phoney, but if you were getting some, I was like, okay. And you can't tell shit to somebody in love. So, I saw it coming. A lot of people did. You just didn't, because you're decent. But now you have to just face it. Fucking hate her guts, burn her pictures, get a girlfriend who's twice as hot and rub her face in it." She looked straight ahead at the pools of light the headlights cast on the brush at the edge of the pulloff.

He sucked air and looked out the window.

"What about Amanda Pedesky? She's liked you for like five

years. She's completely built, like, supercute."

He thought about Meghan's breath after they smoked pot, how he could smell it in her sweat when they made love afterwards.

"I'd totally hit that shit if I were you." She looked at him to see if he was rising to the bait. "Or why don't you finally fucking ask Marissa Berns out? I swear that ass can't be real, but you have a better chance of finding out than I do."

"Don't you get tired of scamming on straight girls?" he said, flattered but uncomfortable with her knowing, knowing that now she would expect him to do something, to denounce Meaghan, to give up hope.

"If you didn't hide in your fucking bat cave all the time, you'd know that I am officially almost getting laid. And, she goes to our school. And, she is fucking hot."

"Who?"

"I don't know if I want to tell you."

"Afraid it will queer things?"

She grinned and put the truck in drive. He kept going. "Just be straight with me." They both grinned wider. He said, "I'm trying to think of one with 'dyke' in it but I can't."

"You're a total dork," she said and threw her arm out to the right, grazing his shoulder with her fist and driving her elbow into the dusty seat back between them. She let a few moments pass and said, "I'm worried about you. You know, staying here, next fall. Not, like, doing anything."

Jack shrugged. "You and Jeremy are smart. It isn't . . . you just have . . . it isn't like any colleges are going to take me. I'm just, like, regular."

"You always say that: 'I'm a regular guy.' It's not really true. I mean, Jeremy is brilliant, and I kick fucking ass, and you hang. You could totally do communications. Do you know who majors in communications? Fucking football players and wrestlers. I'll bet you could learn computers. You and Jeremy geek out. I mean, seriously, this is shit you're fucking great at. What the fuck? Try it."

He shifted in his seat and said, "Maybe I'll go to Community."

"Sorry, I feel like I'm yelling at you."

"It's all right," he said. "So who is she?"

"Your mom," she said.

93

"Stop it, you're turning me on," he said.

"Promise you won't tell?"

"Okay."

"Cross your heart?"

"I don't want to know anymore. Fuck you."

"Brandy fucking Whitlock."

"No shit."

"No shit."

"Dude, high five." She smacked his hand without looking away from the windshield. "How did that happen?"

"She just came up and told me I was so butch I turned her gay."

"Seriously. Brandy is gay for you?"

"She just came up and told me she thought about girls, like thought about girls, and then she told me she thought about me, and would I like to go to the coffeehouse with her and hang out."

"And you almost fucked her?"

"No, douche, I just hung out with her. She's really nice."

"And that's 'almost laid'?"

"For me it is, asshole. I can't wait to get the fuck out of here, Jack. I've pretty much been gay for three years, and I can't ask girls out, because no matter how good your gaydar is you can't depend on a girl's reaction."

"Duh."

"Not just, like, rejection. It's like you made them hate themselves by asking them or something, so then they hate you."

"But now you have Brandy. Maybe. Hopefully."

She thumped the steering wheel with her hand and said, "No, dude, that's . . . you can't think that way. That's like, this part of my life is ending, not, like looking forward. Like it's time to settle down and shit. You're trying to be old. We're not old. We're stupid fucking kids." She thumped the steering wheel again, then said, "Want to get high?"

"Seriously?"

"Yeah. But we should pick up Jeremy first."

Jack smoked Marlboros with his arm held just out the window, inhaling the wet leaf smell of the wooded ravines, and wished she were riding beside him.

Meaghan called the Sunday before Thanksgiving. Jack was home alone, playing a port of Atari Space Invaders for PC that he had downloaded. He paused his game and picked up without checking the caller ID box. She said, "Hello," and the air left his lungs. He coughed and said, "Hi," and sat down. He reached in his pockets for a cigarette and lit it. "Meaghan?"

"Yeah," she said, drawing the word out, and he could see her crooked smile. "You haven't called in a while. I was worried you'd forgotten me."

He wondered if she was making fun of him. "I didn't. I. Uh."

"I was wondering if you'd drive into Pittsburgh and pick me up at the bus station. I'm taking the Long Dog home."

"I could. Sure, I guess."

"Sweet. I can't wait to see you honey. I'm getting in at eight on Tuesday night. It's right near the, whatchacallit, the convention center."

He said nothing to his parents, and made sure he didn't mention Meaghan at all to Abbi or Jeremy, who kept coming up with names of girls he should ask out. His parents planned a bonfire for Wednesday night, and invited his friends before he could think of a way to stop them. On Tuesday he showered, lied to his mother, and drove through the tunnels into downtown under heavy skies. The roads seemed to pull him towards the bus depot, and he sat in the pickup area, smoking and watching flurries fall for half an hour before he saw her wrestling a huge duffel bag to the curb. He helped her toss it over the side of the truck, and she threw her arms around him, and then her mouth was warm and wet on his. He moved his arms to embrace her and buried his face in her thick black hair.

In the truck she talked nonstop, but the sound she made was the roar of pounding surf, the rush of blood. Staring forward at the road, he realized he'd agreed to take her out on Wednesday, that he'd told her about the bonfire. "I wish we could go somewhere and get all caught up," she said, "but my grandma is staying at our house so she can see me tonight, and I have to go home." He drove the highway, took the exit that dumped them off in Bridgeville, and took back roads to her house. He hoped she'd kiss him good night, but she just kissed her hand and blew it at him, grinned, and dragged her duffel to her door.

She called him the next morning and his mom answered the phone. Her face contorted when she heard Meaghan's voice, but she said, "Here he is" and put him on. She stood looking worried at him for a few more moments, and then turned to leave and give him his privacy. He said, "Hello," and she said, "Hi, Jackanapes. Why don't you pick me up and take me to lunch?"

He drove to her house, where she was waiting out front, dressed in a tight gray wool dress and knee-high leather boots, her hair glossy-black over a red leather jacket. She hopped into the cab and leaned over to kiss him on the cheek.

He took her to Applebee's, where they split potato skins and jalapeno poppers, and she talked about her play and all of the people in the drama program, the totally sexy professor who ran the show, the sexy sensitive ex-marine who played the villain, the sexy black guy who played the wise prince, the sexy director, and the sexy guy who made the sets. She looked at him and said, "You're quiet, even for you, Jack. Is everything okay?"

He looked down at the huge lump of sour cream on the otherwise empty potato skins platter and said, "I guess, yeah."

"Come on, Jack. What's up?"

He wondered if she was just nuts, but also wondered if he was, too. "I just . . . I really missed you," he said, getting choked up. He watched her watch a tall man with long stringy hair, wearing tight jeans and a shirt slit open at the sides to show off his ribs, walk through the restaurant.

"I missed you, too," she said, and when they finished eating she let him pick up the check. He followed her around the mall, waiting outside of dressing rooms as she paraded outfits in front of him. They stopped at a cigar store to buy cigarettes, and Jack smoked a butt with the owner, who introduced himself as Mister Antonelli, and had him fill out an application. When he read it, he said, "Grappa, huh?" and gave him a free cigar for being Italian.

It rained softly as the sun set, but they could tell it wouldn't last long. She told him about a party in the woods. "We could go, just for a while, then go to your parents'," she said. "They won't care."

Jack pulled the truck down a long access road and parked when he saw cars abandoned halfway in the ditch. They walked up the narrow path, smelled the fire, heard voices in the dark. Over a small rise they saw the party, sixty or seventy kids, drinking bottles and cans, smoking water bongs made from two-liter soda bottles or PVC pipe.

Three guys Jack recognized from the yearbook video came up to them and talked to Meaghan, offering her a drink. She kissed one of them warmly on the cheek. When she asked if Jack could have one too, they looked at him as if he weren't there, and kept talking as if they hadn't heard her. He walked up to a cooler and took a beer for himself. Immediately a red-faced kid with bad skin and a crew cut grabbed it from him and said, "What the fuck? It's bring your own, motherfucker." One of the guys who was talking to Meaghan came over and said something to the guy, who handed Jack his beer and walked away. Jack popped it open and chugged it, then dropped the can and took another. He looked around but couldn't see where Meaghan had gone.

He borrowed a lighter from a sophomore girl and lit his cigar. It was hard not to inhale, but he liked the taste, liked the idea of being the weirdo smoking a big cigar at a party. The girl said her name was Irene, and asked him how the video yearbook was coming together. She was slim, with big eyes and high cheekbones, and Jack suddenly wished he were at the party alone. He repeated her name to himself. Another girl stumbled up and said, "Jack Grappa! Are you going to put me in your movie?" After a while the cigar got old, so he threw it in the fire. He knew he had to leave, and the girl named Irene asked him if he had come with Meaghan. She said, "I mean, I saw she was here."

"Yeah," he said. "She came with me."

"It's really cool that you two are friends still," she said. He looked around, politely excused himself from the group of younger students who had gathered around him, and walked the party, looking for her hair and listening for her laugh.

After a couple of turns around the circle, he found her sitting with the guy she had kissed hello, off to the side. He stood in front of her and said, "We have to go, my folks are waiting for us."

"Easy there, buddy," the other boy said.

Jack glared into his shadow. Meaghan said, "I have to go, but I'm definitely . . . I'll call you," and he followed her towards the truck. Back in the cab, she said "Jack, are you jealous again?"

He started the engine and flipped on the lights.

"You are! You're jealous. She looked forward through the windshield. "I have to keep reminding myself you're still just a kid."

He had nothing to say to that; he didn't want to be anywhere near her, but also wondered if she would still have sex with him.

Halfway to her house, she unbuckled her seatbelt and hiked up her skirt. He smelled whiskey on her, the way it was a different smell on her than on his dad or anyone else. She tossed something at his face, and he grabbed it from his lap, realized it was her thong. He turned down the driveway of a deserted house and killed his headlights, pulling out behind the old garage, their place. He took off his pants and she lay back on the bench seat. He lowered himself on top of her, took great sleek handfuls of her hair, kissed her and rubbed himself on her, feeling her legs open wider. She gasped, and he felt the power of making her gasp, the feeling that whatever else loomed before him, he could do this one thing well: love her, make love to her. He reached down and righted the angle, and began working himself inside her. She arched her back and sighed softly, then snapped her eyes open and said, "No!" She wiggled him out of her, pulled herself upright in the cab of the truck. He thought she wanted head, and started to press his mouth to her belly, but she pulled back so violently her knee cracked his jaw. He sat up and pulled back as she re-arranged her skirts. He said, "What the fuck?"

"It's just, we shouldn't, Jack."

"Why not?"

"Jack, just—no, okay. I don't need a reason. No. Things are different now. No."

"I guess I'm too fucking immature to get it," he said, and started to shove his legs back into his jeans. She was quiet. He drove like a maniac, fishtailing through curves, not wanting her to see him cry.

She said, "Now you're mad," and he didn't answer her. He looked out the side mirror while she got out of his truck, and turned up the radio when she tried to say goodbye. He burned tire out of her parents' driveway and went and sat on the old stone bridge on Sumac Road, watching the black water fifty feet below shoot across the smooth boulders at the foot of the pilings. He cried and wondered how quick it would be, how much he would feel, and he wanted to do it, because it couldn't be worse than feeling this way. He spit once, then again, watching it drop into blackness and rushing water.

It was cold and damp on top of the bridge, and he got back in his truck and went home. Jeremy's car was still in the driveway, and he went around to the back of the house. They all stopped talking and turned towards him, but he couldn't see their faces in the shadows cast by the fire. Jack walked up to a blue plastic ice chest and opened the grimy white lid, took a flavored vodka cooler and twisted off the cap with his shirttail. Jack's dad tossed his cigarette into the remains of the bonfire and said, "Well, goodnight, ladies and gents." He picked up his glass, leaned down to lay his palm on Jack's head, and went in through the cellar door. Jack's mom didn't say a word, but she locked eyes with Abbi, and Jack thought he saw her give a curt nod. She gathered up bottles and plasticware and followed her husband inside.

Jack sat with his friends on the hillside at the back of his house, smoking in silence. Jeremy produced a joint, and after they had smoked it, he lay on the grass humming a tuneless medley of Led Zeppelin songs. Abbi said, "Your parents threw you a party, dickhead."

"Don't," he said. "Just don't."

"Fuck, Jack," she said. "I'm serious. You fucked up."

"I don't want to hear it. I can't deal with it right now." He felt the world spin a little.

She said, "It's one thing if you're going to lock yourself in a room and mope, but when you start blowing us off—me, Jeremy, and your fucking parents. Bullshit, Jack!" She stood up and glared at him. "I'm done talking to you. I'm going to bed." She went in through the cellar door, and he could see her making up the downstairs couch with sheets his mother had left for her.

Jack helped Jeremy inside and got him into the recliner, took off his sneakers and pulled a blanket over his legs. Abbi pretended to be asleep a few feet away.

Jeremy blinked open his eyes and settled a drunken smile on

Jack. He whispered, "Yo, buddy, did you get any?" and offered Jack a low five on the sly.

Dreamland

Emilie knows she is grinning like a pumpkin-headed fool, feels the ache of happiness at the corners of her mouth. Philip sits on the dog-hair recliner, meeting her mom. Her mom beams back from the couch with a pumpkin-head grin of her own, and she is not that far into the Carlo Rossi. Emilie pours a dirty tumbler of Fat Dago for herself and one for Philip, who tries, God love him, to pet Magoo, the Lhasa Apso with the skin condition. She finds his awkwardness touching, and she tells herself she does not have to be ashamed of the dog-hair recliner or the brown Christmas tree by the window or the dog-pee fruit-fly smell of their apartment, or her nervous fry-headed mom, who downs her tumbler of Carlo Rossi and swirls her glass for Emilie to refill.

"So my daughter," Donna says, placing a theatrical hand on Emilie's wrist as she takes her drink, "My daughter says you're a teacher."

"Yes, Mrs. Deluca, I teach band at Oakdale Area."

Donna beams at him, then turns to beam at Emilie. "And, ah, my daughter says you wanted to talk to me about something." She looks like her head will pop from smiling, and Emilie feels a little headache coming on.

"Well," the young man stutters, "I—first, I want you to understand. Nothing inappropriate has happened between me and your daughter. We held hands, but we haven't even kissed or anything. And, I mean, we haven't—we aren't going to, uh, touch, until she's eighteen. Until she's out of school. But we, we like have this connection."

Donna says. "How old are you?"

"Uh, twenty-three," Philip says, squirming. Emilie loves him; she is bursting with love.

Her mother squeals, "Oooooo, Mon Emilie, he's just perfect. An older boy, an educated boy. Where did you go to school?"

"U. Pitt Johnstown." Philip relaxes a little, rolling his shoulders forward, taking a belt off of the dirty tumbler of Fat Dago. "It's just, we have this connection." He looks over at Emilie and they lock eyes, and he starts to grin a purple-toothed grin. His relief washes over her; now there is just the space of months before she graduates.

"Soooooo, so, so romantic," Donna says, twirling her glass for more Carlo Rossi. "You two kids are going to be so happy, so happy. Oh, Emilie," she says, making soft clucking sounds. "Oh Emilie, oh Emilie, oh you're growing up. I'm going to cry!" She sobs, her shoulders rolling and heaving, the wine splashing Poughkeepsie the Pekinese. Emilie hands her some Kleenex, and Donna dries her eyes.

They leave her to sleep it off as the ten o'clock news flickers on the TV, and Emilie walks Philip to his car. She feels the gap of space between them like a ring of fire. She wants him to be her first time, and they will have to wait most of a school year. She can't stand it, suddenly, and she wraps her arms around his middle and sobs into his shirt, "I want you! I want you!" He wraps his skinny arms around her and stammers, "I want you, too." She kisses him, a long, wet, fleshy kiss, and Emilie is shocked at herself. She has never kissed anyone for real before.

"I want to take you away from this. I promise. Oh shit!"

Because there she is, the fucking wonder bitch, Ms. Caster, parked across the street, stalking them, emerging from her little Honda, coming toward them, ruining their embrace and the heart-pounding feelings she is having being so close to him.

"Idiot!" Ms. Caster says. "Idiot! What are you trying to do to yourself?" Emilie knows Ms. Caster hates her. Ms. Caster used to jerk Philip around like a dog on a leash, until they had a fight and he dumped her. He told Emilie about it after band practice, when they were alone, at the beginning of September, when she started bumping into him accidentally-on-purpose during their free periods. He told her that Ms. Caster was his first real girlfriend. He said that she was the kind of woman who would castrate a man, and Emilie told him she would never do that, and he said, "I know," because it is like he can see inside her soul. Now the leaves are full gold and it is nearly dark by seven thirty, and he is Emilie's man. She longs to feel like she is his woman, to hold him and to be held, and she is jealous of Ms. Caster because Ms. Caster has been in Philip's arms and she doesn't deserve to have been. Emilie bristles and thinks about trying to smash in Ms. Caster's buck teeth.

Ms. Caster stands in front of them, and Philip draws back, disentangling himself from Emilie's embrace. Emilie glares at Ms. Caster, tears at the edge of her anger. She thinks that she will fight for her man, and she remembers an old Loretta Lynn song about gunning down the low-class floozy who wants to break up her family.

"You're going to get fired, you know that? You could go to prison!"

Emilie blurts out, "He hasn't done anything! We haven't done anything. So you leave him alone, you horrible old troll."

Ms. Caster glares back at Emilie, and Emilie is scared of her pointy-bra boobs and her thin-lipped sneer, of what she could do to her and to Philip. She pushes closer and closer to Emilie, and she feels less and less like a feisty coal miner's daughter, and more like a rabbit in the headlights. "Go home, Emilie. Go inside, little girl. Go live your pathetic life and leave him alone. You don't know what you're doing. You can't imagine what you are doing to him."

Philip says, "Emilie, let me—just go ahead. We'll talk tomorrow." He angles himself towards her and mouths, "It's okay." Then he rolls his eyes and mouths, "Bitch."

Emilie goes inside and watches out the bathroom window as they argue in the street. Ms. Caster starts crying, and Philip puts his arms around her, and something fills Emilie's throat and her chest and she is wracked with sobs. She wishes Ms. Caster was covered in scabs, wishes she had breast cancer and gangrene and tapeworms and lice. She looks again and they are gone, and she is filled with doubt and a horrible creeping feeling that things are getting worse. After a while, she takes a sweater and goes out again, looking for either of their cars, but they are gone, the troll and her sweet Philip. She walks the four chilly starlit blocks to

May's house and scratches at the screen until the window slides up and May hisses, "Out front!"

May slips out, and they smoke her mom's Winston Lights as they meander back to Emilie's house. When they get there, Emilie's mom has vomited on herself, so the two girls strip her to her bra and panties, throw the wine-stained clothes on the pile in her bedroom, and wash her face with a dish cloth. Then May washes a couple of glasses, and they steal big tumblers of wine, and Emilie tells May all about it for the fifth time as they sit on Emilie's big bed and smoke Winston Lights as Sunday turns to Monday morning.

May sneaks home to sleep for a few hours. In the morning, Emilie is too tired to take a bath, even though it has been a few days and her feet and her crotch and her armpits smell. She is super hungry, and is grateful there is no food in the house. She loves her new flat tummy, the attention she gets now that she has slimmed down. She gets dressed and May picks her up in the old Fiesta that smells like antifreeze.

They walk through the big lower lot towards the doors beside the gym, where May heads to her locker and Emilie cuts through to Philip's office next to the band room. He isn't there, so she heads to class.

She goes to band practice, but Philip isn't there, either. Instead, Ms. Caster leads them through endless loops of "Louie Louie," screeching at May who drops her drumsticks in fright, glaring at Emilie from time to time, letting Emilie know something terrible has happened. Emilie puts her glockenspiel in the equipment room and then goes to the bathroom to puke up the hoagie she had for lunch and cry.

Afterwards May takes her to Philip's house, where they park under a tree and wait for his lights to go on. Instead, Ms. Caster's car pulls up, with Philip in the passenger's seat. They take groceries inside. When he takes out the trash, May shoves her arm and hisses, "Go, go!" but Emilie loses her nerve and just watches his hunched figure retreat, listening to the faint hiss and swoosh and click of the storm door. They sit there for almost an hour when May says, "I'm getting hungry."

May drives her home, and calls her parents to say she's staying over, and May paints while Emilie lies on the dog-hair couch, May saying, "You don't know that" or "Why don't you call him?" or "She is totally a fucking bitch." Emilie sips at her mom's wine.

At nine, Donna comes in with the rattle of keys and the smell of cigarettes in her hair, fumbling with a shopping bag of fresh work clothes. "Ho, my chickadees," she says. "Hiya, May! Are you with us for the long haul?" May nods. "You girls want to run down and get me some smokes?"

So they walk down the hill with a twenty and buy three packs of Marlborough Lights from Manny at the gas station, who flirts with them through an artificial voice box he has to hold up to his throat. On the way back, May says, "Are you going to tell your mom?"

"I hope not."

"I wish you'd had the chance to fuck him. I mean, maybe you still can, but..."

"Me too," she says, and May holds Emilie while she sobs, "I thought someone finally wanted me."

In Emilie's living room, Donna clucks at them, asking how their day went, downing glasses of burgundy. She asks after Philip, and May looks at her feet as Emilie breaks into a loud bawl. Donna sits forward and downs her wine. "What happened? What did he do?"

Emilie tells her about Ms. Caster stalking Philip at their house, and about Philip getting in her car. She leaves out the part about hiding outside his house. Donna says, "I can't believe it!' and "What a scoundrel!" and "I should call the cops, that's what I should do. How dare he? How dare he?" But Emilie talks her out of it. She doesn't want to get Philip in trouble. So she tells her mother that Ms. Caster is blackmailing Philip, that she threatened his job and said she would get him arrested. Donna says, "Oh, that bitch! That fucking bitch! How dare she!"

After Donna passes out, she and May take a mostly-empty bag of sugar and a screwdriver from the corner by the stove and sneak out into the night. Emilie has finished crying, and has a satisfying empty feeling as she and May walk two miles in the shadows on the dead-dark quiet streets of Oakdale. In front of Philip's dingy house is Ms. Caster's car, an asparagus-green Honda, and Emilie is so nervous that May has to walk her into the hedges two doors down so she can pee. They crouch under the hedges and smoke cigarettes, cupping them like soldiers to hide the glowing cherries, their stomachs full of butterflies. May pushes her out into the night, hissing, "Do it! Do it!" She jams the screwdriver in behind the fuel door, put she needs May's help to pry it open. May unscrews the gas cap and Emilie pours in a slim trickle of sugar.

"Do you think that will be enough?" she whispers. May shrugs in the darkness. Emilie takes her house key from her pocket and makes a scratch in the paint, and they run for home, expecting sirens and flashing lights, hearts beating like police helicopters.

But in the morning, Ms. Caster arrives at school in her green Honda with Philip slumped in the passenger seat. Emilie watches from the window outside the second-floor girls' room, sees how unhappy he is, how slowly he moves, and she wants to rescue him. She is both relieved and disappointed that the car isn't wrecked. She thinks that he is the one, really and truly the one, and she doesn't know what to do about the fat, buck-toothed blackmailing tramp who has stolen her one true love.

May makes Emilie watch bad horror films, the badder the better, and she inserts Ms. Caster into the images of make-believe spurting blood and zombie gore, imagines herself with a chainsaw for an arm, hacking at Ms. Caster's shambling undead carcass, blowing her away with her double-barreled shotgun. Emilie stuffs her pockets full of sharpies. She writes "Ms. Caster sucks cocks" in every stall in every girls' bathroom at school. She still wants him. She misses him, and it hurts. She goes back and adds, "and takes it up the butt" to half of her graffiti before she loses interest.

Emilie and May only have one academic class—English—and the rest of their schedule is taken up by band, art, and free periods. They also have wood shop, which is no big deal because Mr. Shea gives girls A's as long as they don't try to touch anything or work with the tools. Emilie and May spend most of every school day drawing, or painting, or making ceramics, or just listening to the radio and hanging out on the carpet in the art room and talking to Mrs. Mastriani, who tells them both that they have real talent.

At Wednesday's band class, Ms. Caster is there again, and

Philip is nowhere to be seen, so Emilie slips out when Ms. Caster goes to the can and goes looking through the half-deserted school for him. She likes the slap of her Chuck Taylors against the institutional tiles in the hard green hallways. She stops to fix her hair in the bathroom mirror, and picks her teeth with her fingernail. She finds him working in Ms. Caster's classroom, marking quizzes. She slips in and closes the door, and he looks startled when he turns to see her.

He stammers, "Emilie!" and she stands with her back to the door, breathing hard. "Emilie—you shouldn't—I can't. She'll see!"

She starts crying, bawling, waiting to feel him put his arms around her, and he does. He says, "Shhh! Shhhh!," and she feels her nose full of snot and blubbers into his grey wool sweater. "I miss you," she says.

"Emilie," he says, "Monica is right. You and I can't do this." She hears him, but pushes herself up, pushes her mouth against his, and as he is knocked back on the desk she kisses him, runs her hands over his scrawny chest and presses herself against his crotch. He is kissing her back and pushing her shoulders away at the same time, and he shoves her away as he regains his footing. His eyes are pleading. "Emilie, I can't. We can't. I wish—but we can't!"

The door opens, and Ms. Caster is boiling. "God dammit, Phillip!' she says.

"I didn't do a thing!" he squeaks.

Through angry tears Emilie says, "Why can't you leave him alone? Why can't you leave us be?"

Ms. Caster moves towards her, seems to tower over her like the evil queen in Snow White, her shoulders up, her white-knuckled hands balled by her sides. "Because I'm not going to let him throw his life away on white trash jailbait. You know why they call girls like you jailbait, right?"

Emilie can't respond, but inside she tries to ignore the click of recognition that, yes, if she gets her way, and anyone tells, Philip will go to prison where they will piss in his food and rape him, just like on HBO. She doesn't care what the world says, though – this is love. If love isn't worth gambling your life on, what is? She sobs, "Why are you so mean?"

Mrs. Caster sighs. "Every silly little girl has crushes. Get over it. Go find yourself a boy your age. But, so help me, if I see you near him again... Well, I better not." Emilie is crying, and Ms. Caster gets her a box of Kleenex. Emilie doesn't want to take anything from her, but she doesn't want to get snot all over herself in front of Philip, so she grabs a handful and throws herself into the corridor, out of the building. She heads for the parking lot and sits next to the bumper of May's Fiesta, leaning her head against the cold chrome when her face feels hot from crying, feeling cold and empty and wishing she were dead.

Emilie is sitting in the dirt crying in the dark when May comes out of drum practice. She holds Emilie and says, "Oh fuck! I'm sorry! I'm so sorry I'm late." She drives Emilie home, but says her mom is expecting her for chore night. Emilie finds Donna passed out with Poughkeepsie on her lap. She pulls the bathrobe down over Donna's panties and sits next to her, making scratching motions on her own leg so that Poughkeepsie will come over. She pours herself a coffee mug of wine and slugs it down like a cowboy. She pours herself another, feels a pleasant burning in her guts. She holds the little dog, scratching him under the chin until he nips her finger and returns to Donna's lap. Donna is snoring, and suddenly Emilie hates her mother, hates herself, hates Philip and Ms. Caster. She thinks about calling May or sneaking over to her house, but walks to the bathroom instead. She finds a half-bottle of Nyquil and chugs it. There is even more Dayquil and she chugs that down, and a hard metallic smell seems to hang on her palate. She looks for her mom's pill stashes; she takes the five pills left in the bottom of the container, lies down on the bathroom floor, and goes to sleep.

Emilie wakes to a horrible chemical smell and her mother shrieking her name: "Emilie! Emilie! Oh, Emilie!" She wakes thinking she is covered in blood, but her panic is held in check by her pounding headache, and she realizes she has puked red wine and cough syrup and she is probably okay. She gags and dry-heaves and says, "Mom, it's okay, it's okay," but Donna makes chicken noises and helps Emilie to clean up and get to bed. Donna calls her in sick to school, then calls off work, cleans Emilie's face with a damp cloth, cleans the bathroom and bangs and clangs through the rest of the house. She washes the dishes, goes to the store, brings back cans of tomato soup and Campbell's chicken and cream of mushroom and Spaghetti-O's, which Emilie sits eating in her bedroom, cold from the can the way she likes them. She rereads some old literature anthologies she skimmed from a box of discards at school the year before, and the copy of Northanger Abbey she straight up stole from the shelves at the back of the English classroom.

On a big piece of butcher paper she is drawing faces from memory: Donna, a little younger, deep scared folds in her face from worry, her dad's big Italian hair and his handsome clown face. She is the lens of the camera; she is six years old and she is sick, and Dave and Donna are worried, and they hold hands and hold each other, and it is before her dad left to go to Connecticut, before he had a girlfriend and a stepdaughter who is a whiny fucked-up bitch who has to wear a wig because she pulls out her own hair. She feels transported in her work, and imagines color; she begins to plan a painting, and so the sketch changes from the thing that is coming into being to a plan for something else. Philip and the troll seem far away, and the happiest day of her life is in charcoal and pencil.

In school a week later, she gessoes a canvas and studies her sketches. She works for a while on one she did of her dad's hands the last time he came to visit. She thinks about dropping band, and has promised herself she won't have anything to do with Phillip the Limpet, who she misses with a cold empty feeling where the promise of love had been. She dreams she is posing for Manet's Olympia, and finds a book about the model for the painting, a woman impressionist left in obscurity by the male-dominated art world. She is dedicating herself to art like a vestal virgin; she wants art to burn her up and make her blow away.

She tries all day in the art room, but the painting doesn't work. The sketch is hardly photorealistic, but it has a stark, grotesque quality that she cannot bring to paint. She walks home with May, who is working on a drawing of a dragon because she is obsessed with The Lord of the Rings. May is an illustrator more than a painter. "I think mine is more your type thing," Emilie tells her. "I want to . . . like, it's a storybook scene. But I'm not that kind of artist."

"What about colored pencil or something?"

"Maybe. Can you come over?"

May shrugs. "Is there anything to eat?"

Emilie says, "We can get chips and stuff. Right now I need to feel like I can do something right. I need your ass."

At the gas station at the bottom of the street they buy salt-and-vinegar chips and Slim Jims and Camel Lights and the old man uses his electronic voicebox to say, "Y'inz girls won't reca-nize the place by spring we're building a minimart n'at an' I'll let your ma know when we're hiring if y'inz want summer jobs n'at." He strings everything together because the first words of sentences get clipped if he pauses, and Emilie and May feel grown-up for being able to follow what he is saying.

Back in the crowded storage room and sometimes-studio, Emilie cranks up the electric radiator, moves some boxes out into the hall, brings in a lamp from the living room, and pulls the shade. May sheds her clothes and stands scratching her butt. "How do you want me?"

Emilie brings in her boom box and plays Simon and Garfunkel's greatest hits. "Lie on your side, turned away from me, like you're asleep. Put your arm under your head. Try to decline your torso a little and get your hips up in the air." As she draws the first few pencil lines on a fresh canvas, Emilie compares her own body to May's. May had been "May-be a boy, May-be a girl" at school the year before, but her bad perm has grown out to reveal sleek straight dark hair. Her legs are long, and her sudden boobs seem to levitate in midair. Emilie looks down her own shirt and ponders her own lopsided little girls, her pear-shaped torso, her short bowlegs. She covers the canvas in what looks like a color field painting—dark oranges and reds, but with the suggestion of curves emanating upwards from an imaginary horizontal line. She sheds her brush and finger-paints some of it, and ends up with an orange-painted nostril when she absentmindedly picks her nose. As she works in spidery black, May's curves emerge, and Emilie puts herself in the place of a man who will someday see her through this lens of fire, approach from behind and kiss her shoulder blades. She thinks about the bodice-ripper novels that she and May trade back and forth, laughs at the idea of Sir Horace Loudwater's heaving chest, wonders how anything so silly can be so painful.

May says, "If you don't feed me, I swear I'm going to sit on you and piss." Emilie takes a thick brush, gobs green paint on the end, and flicks it across May's back.

May snorts as she laughs and says, "Oh my god, you did not just do that." She sits up, and Emilie wipes off the paint, and May gets a joint out of her purse.

"Is that a reefer?" Emilie asks.

"Is that a reefer?" May says, crossing her eyes and making a face.

"Shut up!" Emilie says, but she is giggling already.

"Nobody says 'reefer.'" May lights it and they pass it back and forth.

"Where did you get it?"

"Billy McMullen wants to fuck me. He just walked up and gave it to me and told me there's plenty more where that comes from. He thinks he's a gangsta."

Emilie holds in her smoke and says, "He's kind of cute."

May shrugs. "Not my type. He's all skinny. And I think my dad might have done his mom at some point. My mom hates his mom. So that's weird. He told me I have a fly bootie." Both girls giggle like they are six years old.

Donna opens the door, pokes her head in, shrieks and pulls her head back into the hallway like a turtle. Emilie opens the door while her mom makes chicken noises and says, "Do you want a toke, mommy?"

"You girls! I don't know how I feel about you playing around with that stuff under my roof. And May in her birthday suit! You're like a bunch of beatniks, running wild like a bunch of hottentots!"

May and Emilie shriek with laughter. "Hottentots!" May giggles.

"Beatniks!" Emilie snorts back.

Donna looks at the smoldering joint and says, "Maybe just a little to help with my, ah," and she hits the joint like a champion while both girls watch in open-mouthed amazement. She hits it again and again, and the Emilie says, "You have to share, Ma," and Donna looks hungry as they take their turns. May puts her clothes on and they drive to Applebee's, where the girls split nachos and a hot fudge brownie sundae and Donna gets bombed on two-for-one frozen margaritas and throws up lime green in the parking lot. May helps clean Donna up and then Emilie drives them home.

When it is dry, Emilie brings the painting to school to show Mrs. Mastriani. Sitting on a machinist's stool by the big steel-sash windows the old woman whistles. "Emilie," she says, "This is impressive. You should enter it." She is talking about a contest sponsored by LaRoche College in the North Hills. LaRoche is where Will Negrete went. Will Negrete with the long eyelashes and the long pale fingers; Emilie fantasizes about running into him at the student art show. Emilie leaves the painting with Mrs. Mastriani.

She wants to show her painting to Philip, and she starts to go to the back of the band room where he has his office. But she is there, and he hears them talking about the spring musical, and Emilie turns and scuttles away. She hates Ms. Caster, and she wonders if she can get over Philip, and thinks how unfair it is that she should have to. She can't understand how he could pick Ms. Caster over her. She feels like Philip is a pathetic douche. And, she misses him.

In November, Donna's old bomber won't pass state inspection, so she trades it in on a silver Honda, and she and Emilie dress up for the Nutcracker, and drive to The Cheese Cellar in Station Square. They drive by the Hooters and the big sports bar owned by one of the Steelers, to a parking lot with a toll booth, and they go into the old train station that was turned into a restaurant by a man who was later lost at sea. They run their hands over the old marble and gaze up at the stained glass galleries and eat a raw oyster apiece, Donna downing a couple of Bloody Marys and buying Emilie her favorite, a Virgin Mary with lots of pepper and horseradish and hot sauce.

They move on to The Cheese Cellar, a wine bar where a flamingly gay waiter fawns on them. He floats on pointed toes when they tell him they are headed for the ballet, telling them that he was a dance major at Pitt, then filling them in on gossip about people they do not know. Emilie dunks things into her fondue and giggles with the waiter, feeling far away from their dog-pee living room, while Donna drinks a bottle and a half of white zinfandel.

Emilie sees Donna's switch flip in the car. When they arrive at the ballet, she helps her doddering ma out of the seatbelt and then the door. Donna's legs keep going out from under her, and she doesn't say anything, but she can't seem to let go of the car without jerking and stumbling. Emilie gives the keys to a humongous man who tries not to look at her mother. Donna is hiccoughing and has to leans heavily on Emilie, and Emilie gets her to smoke a cigarette while snooty women glare at them as they pass with little girls in nice dresses, going to the Nutcracker. Emilie takes Donna's credit card to the shiny metal kiosk and gets their tickets, signing her mother's name as Donna hangs on her arm and weeps softly. Emilie steers her inside, where she comes alive long enough to order a plastic glass of white wine, and grumbles at the concessions clerk when she tells them that alcohol is not served at the children's shows. An old woman wearing a brass "Usher" badge gives them a program and a dirty look as Emilie steers Donna to a seat, smelling the stale-perfume smell of white zin on her mother's skin, and she thinks, once she is sitting down, Donna will be okay.

Donna sinks into the theater seat and passes out. Emilie looks around, and sees half-turned-away faces, smirks, and a few little bun-headed ballet girls staring at her mother's worn-out face. The lights go down, and Emilie feels relief like a warm blanket until Donna starts to snore mid-way through the Petite Overture. She elbows her mother, but Donna lets out a loud cry, then settles back in, her head back in an open-mouthed freight-train snore. People are shifting in the seats around her, but Emilie concentrates on the movements of the dancers and thinks about Matisse. She is lost in the show, wishing she had a sketch pad or a camera, that she does not notice the very slender man who is standing behind them, Ichabod-Craned over the back of their seats. He is so thin and tall he seems to have been specially made for his job, which is scooting to the middle of rows in the theater and asking people to leave.

He looks at Emilie and whispers, "I'm telling you as a courtesy, miss: if you don't get her out of here, we're going to have her removed." The people in her aisle file out, and now half the theater is watching as Emilie's mother is cajoled to her feet and given the Baum's rush.

In the lobby, the man says, not unkindly, "Can I call you a cab? Do you think she needs an ambulance?"

Emilie likes him. She says, "No, it's—it's just my mom." He gives her a wan smile, and she says, "She works really hard."

Donna opens her eyes and pitches her head forward in a loll and says, "You fucking cunts can fug shihhh."

Emilie looks at him and says, "We're not really white trash." Before it gets any worse she steers Donna outside, where fat snowflakes are falling in the marquee lights and the cold air wakes Donna up a little for the walk to the car. She sobs, "I'm a bad mother" into Emilie's coat and blows her nose on her glove. Emilie cries while she is driving across the Fort Pitt Bridge, but still tries to hold her breath through the tunnel. She scoops her mom out of the car and gets her as far as the front steps when Donna begins wailing. She throws herself down on the white-dusted pine needles and weeps. She says, "I'm a bad mother. I am. I'm a bad mother."

Emilie says, "No you're not, Mom."

"I'm bad, I'm so bad."

"You're a good mother, Mom. You just like to have some drinky-poos."

"But – NO!"

"Come inside and we'll have a drinky-poo," Emilie croons, and her mother picks herself up, and climbs the front steps. Emilie gets the door open, and Donna heads for the living room with the dead Christmas tree and the smell of dog pee. They pick up Poughkeepsie and Magoo so the dogs can lick their faces. Emilie pours some jug wine in a dirty glass, and Donna takes a sip before she passes out again. Emilie finishes the glass and drinks another. In her head, she keeps replaying Philip's promise to take her away from "all of this," and keeps hearing Ms. Castor calling her "little white trash girl." She drinks a third, goes to the bathroom to puke, brushes her teeth and washes out her mouth with her mother's Scope, and goes to bed.

Emilie calls herself in sick to school for a couple of days, hiding under the blankets and getting up only to do her business and smoke her mother's cigarettes, but she knows that if she malingers too long she will have to get a doctor's note to go back at all, so she takes a bath in the dirty claw-foot tub and May drives her back to the tan cube-like building.

She hides from band, knowing that Philip will not flunk her, and makes a bunch of polymer clay figures, thinking about a Smithsonian article she read that said Giacometti's work from all of the years he spent in Switzerland could fit inside a suitcase. The miniatures are fun, and she even makes a miniature Don Quixote as an homage, but then she wants to work bigger. She begins to regret blowing off wood shop and metal shop, but thinks that she wouldn't be wanted there anyway, and so she blames the shop teacher and the burnout boys who are hostile towards girls like her, and she starts making ceramic sculptures that look like hills and buildings from Dr. Seuss books.

Mrs. Mastriani goes out to get the mail, and comes back with a sheet of red-embossed letterhead. "Emilie!" she says, "You're a finalist! Congratulations!" Emilie and May take turns hugging the short, chubby old woman.

As the day ticks by, Emilie wishes more and more that she could share this with Philip; she feels like he is her muse, even when, or especially because, he causes her pain. She thinks of the way her mother loves her father—they still sleep together when he comes to visit every few years—and wonders if there is nothing in the world but pain.

She is training herself to eat less, and she takes a little pleasure in the rumble of her empty stomach. When it gets to be too much, and even smoking isn't enough, she drinks coffee with cream and sugar.

She decides not to skip band, and she sits at the back and waits. When he comes through the door at the front of the room, she feels the greenish florescent lights dim. He sees her and half-waves and swallows and looks away. She slips out past Delia Rosen, who is coming in late with her alto sax, Emilie's eyes wet, her wide, thick-lipped mouth frozen in an ugly sneer of grief as she sobs. She makes it to the girl's room without running into anyone, and she locks herself in a stall and cries. When she is all cried out, she reads her graffiti. Someone has drawn stick figures, one fellating the other, and labeled them "Ms. Caster" and "Mr.

Weigel" —Philip. She finds a coin in her pocket and scratches at the image until she has worn away some of the paint around it.

She tries twice more to go to band, but she can't stay. She tells May that it is like being kicked in the chest. So she spends even more time in the art room, drawing from magazine photographs and listening to Howard Stern on the radio.

Emilie does a speech on Manet for English class, and May does hers on Monet, figuring that people should be made aware of the fact that they are two different painters. Emilie talks for twenty minutes, fielding a few questions at the end. May mumbles the whole thing into her paper, and when she sits down she hides her face in her hair so that it falls away from her bright-red ears, and Emilie follows her to the bathroom and holds her while she shakes and cries through a panic attack.

Safely back in the art room, Mrs. Mastriani gathers them in her arms and squeezes and says, "Emilie, you won! You won!"

Mrs. Mastriani reads her the letter, and she and May pass it back and forth. Emilie feels herself warm to the glow of recognition.

On the Saturday before Christmas break, Emilie drives May up 79 to the North Hills, crosses McKnight Road and sails up the driveway to the big crowded student lot at LaRoche College. The girls walk around a little, looking for college boys, but the wind is blowing hard so they head inside and look for the art show. Emilie's painting, which she decided to call "Dreamland," has taken first place out of over 1200 applicants. She has the letter from Sister Patience Vella pressed inside a copy of Love in the Time of Cholera, in her giant lime green vinyl purse.

They enter a low sprawling brick building that looks like a high school, and walk quietly by the chapel, following taped-up signs that say "Art Show." They walk slowly by the classrooms, which look like high school classrooms, and look at the college kids taking notes or sprawled sleeping in their seats, just like high school. Class lets out at ten minutes to four, and the corridors fill with soccer players and punk rockers. Emilie keeps looking for Will Negrete, and boys keep looking at May.

The girls walk through a labyrinth of cubicle panels hung with line drawings of puppies and acrylics of sports gear leaning against walls and lockers. Emilie finds most of them boring, the kind of stuff that makes her imagine that any of the praise her work gets is just adults pandering to a creative child. There are a few pieces that she does like. One drawing shows an obsessively detailed ripple in an abstracted pond, and she is impressed. Another is an acrylic of a burl on the side of a tree trunk, a piece that uses papier mache to literally leave the canvas and form a crusty glob that she thinks gives an eerie photorealistic impression while remaining abstract.

What she doesn't find is her painting. There is a tag with her name on one of the walls beneath a blank space, but no painting. May says, "You should go find Sister Whatserface."

"I'm Sister Whatserface," says a voice behind them, and as they turn an older woman with bristly salt-and-pepper hair smiles at them and says, "Are you Emilie? I'm Sister Patience." She is wearing a long hippy skirt and a denim jacket, and a button that says, "Pro Woman, Pro Child, Pro Choice" and another that is just a purple triangle and the words "End Hate." Emilie admires her orange leather clogs.

Emilie introduces May, and Sister Patience shakes May's hand. She looks back at Emilie and says, "I'm afraid I have some bad news for you."

"Did something happen to my painting?" Emilie asks, feeling a sudden sense of loss.

"No, no, it's locked in my office. The thing is," she sighs and tents her hands together under her chin, "well, the thing is it's bullshit, but they won't let me hang it. I guess something in the rules says you can't draw people, specifically nudes. It's a disgrace for an art show at an art college, really, and I made a stink about it, but it's been pointed out to me that it's a high school art show, and apparently people are still threatened by the female nude. The long and the short of it is, they can't override my decision as judge, but I'm not allowed to hang your painting."

May pipes up, "That's fucking bullshit!" and Sister Patience says, "Yes, exactly. I told them it's an abstract!" She looks back to Emilie and says, "I wish I could do more, but I fought for you to be able to keep first place so you will have it for your college applications. And I hope you won't hold this against LaRoche; generally we're not this uptight. Any time you deal with high schools it gets political." She waves her hands as if fanning away a bad smell. "Have you thought about where you're going to apply?"

"No. Not really."

"Are you a junior or a senior?"

"Senior."

"Well, you're way behind. Have you thought about college at all?" Emilie shrugs. "Did you take the SAT? Are your grades good?" Emilie nods. She thinks Sister Patience is the coolest nun she has ever heard of. "Well, you should go to college. Otherwise you'll get knocked up and wish you had."

Emilie stares at Sister Patience with open-mouthed awe. She squeaks, "I would love to go to an art school."

Sister Patience says, "We'd love to have such a talented young woman here. We'd be lucky to get you, assuming your grades are good." Emilie nods enthusiastically. "Well, you should give us a look, and go up to Slippery Rock. They have a good program, too. Try Pitt and CMU. If you can't afford the fees, you can ask any of the schools to waive them for need. Don't assume you can't afford it, and don't stop painting. If you come here, look me up. I know some tricks for finding money for deserving students. Come up to my office. You should take your painting home for your portfolio."

Emilie sits behind the wheel of the Honda, but doesn't turn the key. May says, "This fucking sucks."

Emilie says, "Maybe not. I don't know. I think I'm kind of happy and excited. I think it's a silver lining"

"Getting gypped?"

"No, I mean, I think I want to go to college."

May says, "My parents are on me about it, but I don't know. I don't know what I want to do."

"That's what college is for, though," Emilie says.

May shrugs. "I'd go if you went." Emilie knows May is painfully shy around new people and terrified of being alone. When they were twelve, Emilie spent an entire summer reassuring May that she wasn't retarded.

Emilie drives to Eat'n Park and they split a huge chocolate sundae for dinner, and talk about college as if it is a real thing.

Emilie books a tour of LaRoche in early February, but keeps it a secret from her mother. May's mother is excited that she is interested in college, and likes that it is a religious school, even though May's family are not the least bit religious. She has to fight bitterly to make her mother stay at home, and she cries and says she will not go if her mom tries to go with her. Her dad says, "What the hell does a girl need to go to college for?" May tells Emilie everything, and she hates her parents and can't wait to get away from them.

The girls leave early on a Friday morning, and everything is hard-frozen light, Ansel Adams meets Tim Burton. The sun on the wind-polished median strip has them squinting like rats. Emilie speeds along, and May promises to shout "Bacon!" if she sees a state trooper.

Their tour guide, Britney, is bottle-blonde and talks to them like they are six, or talks past them like they aren't there. Every sentence she speaks ends on an upnote, and she can't stop playing with her bangs. Emilie sees a pack of punk-rock art kids from a distance, but the girl shows them the chapel. She takes them to the cafeteria after the noon rush, and the school buys them lunch, and they think they will get to meet some interesting kids, but the place is mostly empty. Britney says "We don't have frats or sororities yet, which sucks, but we're totally supposed to be getting a football team, at least." She's the president of the campus pro-life organization, Heartbeat, and Emilie and May hate her.

They meet with a woman in admissions who wears a cream-colored suit and who asks them questions like "Where do you see yourself in ten years?" and "What are you looking for in a college?" Emilie says, "Having a show in a big art gallery" and "A place to grow." May says, "Well, I hope I can find a job that doesn't totally suck" and "What she said. A place to grow." The woman doesn't seem to care about their answers, and she tells them about the number of LaRoche graphic designers who get jobs after graduation, and about the money coming in that is being used to renovate the whole campus. She offers them a chance to sit in on a sculpture class or graphic design, and before Emilie can say anything, May says, "I want to see what, like,

119

graphic design is all about."

Emilie thinks about protesting but doesn't, so they sit in on a design class, and Emilie bristles as the professor explains an advertising design project, stews as she watches an aloof, kind-of goth girl move her mouse around the screen and try to copy the design elements of a Spanish Civil War propaganda poster and turn it into an ad for Altoids. May sits at one of the computers and a chubby boy with a blue Mohawk shows her some moves on Quark, but Emilie doesn't like the way the place feels.

In the car, May says, "I could totally come here. That guy was cute. And, like, graphic design is something I could do, I think. And my mom and dad would have to buy me a computer."

Emilie says, "It's all about getting a job with these people. It's all graphic design, graphic design. I want to go to an art school." Emilie is upset, and suddenly feels like she might cry. "I think this place would ruin me."

May says, "I think I might be—well, I'm not an artist. But I like computers, and I like art. But if you don't want to go here, we can go somewhere else." She sounds disappointed.

Emilie says, "You don't have to go where I go," but she doesn't mean it.

May calls Slippery Rock, and books them a campus tour on April first, but her parents balk at letting her spend the night in the dorm, so they have to do whole thing in one day. The night before, they comb their sketchbooks and debate paintings, stealing red wine from Donna and a whole pack of Winston Lights from May's mom's carton in the fridge.

It is warm and foggy, and someone has used window chalk to draw a cock and write "slutmobile" on the back window of the Civic. They leave it there—who cares about these Oakdale losers? —and get the fuck out of Dodge.

On 79 north, May shouts "Bacon!" just in time, and Emilie stares into her mirror at the Pennsylvania state police cruiser tucked away in the bushes.

They stop for breakfast at an Eat'n Park, where Emilie eats a big mushroom omelet with ketchup and hot sauce, and leaves May eating pancakes to go puke it up.

When she gets back to the table, May says, "You okay?" and

Emilie shrugs and says "nerves."

They get to Slippery Rock and look out over the campus from a parking lot high on a hill near the glass-and-stone admissions office. May says, "Let's just walk around for a while. They don't know we're here yet. Let's just look around."

Emilie suspects that May is hoping to meet boys, but decides that's not the worst idea she's ever heard. They follow signs to the Student Union, and dodge splatters of bird shit that seem everywhere—sidewalks, buildings, cars. Emilie hears a gaggle of low-flying Canadian honkers, and looks up at them in time to get half a squirt of milky white in her hair.

May guides Emilie to a public restroom and helps her clean up, Emilie dry-heaving and crying. When May has balled up a pile of soiled paper towels, Emilie says, "I don't like it here. I want to go home."

May looks at her and throws her shoulders forward and down in a full-body little-kid pout. She sneers, "We just got here."

Emilie says nothing. She knows she is being unreasonable, but she also feels herself at the edge of a precipice. She feels her dog-pee living room, feels the nights watching her mother pass out on the couch. It is not one specific thing; she feels like a fraud.

May growls, and it is a tone Emilie has never heard before. "You're always sick. You always have a reason for not doing things."

"You can do it without me," Emilie says, and then they are silent because they both know it is not true. "Okay, I'll go on the stupid tour."

They are late, but the lady at admissions is friendly and nice. She talks to them as she wipes her high heels down with some kind of pre-moistened towelette. She says to call her Marcia, and she introduces them to Samantha, who is going to show them around.

Samantha has long black hair and perfect cheekbones, and is small and slim in tight slacks and a v-neck shirt with ruffles that Emilie thinks she could never pull off. She says to call her "Sam," and she is so beautiful and so elegant that the girls are starstruck. Sam tells them that she graduated the year before from the visual arts program, and asks them if they are artists. May says "No, not like an artist or anything." Emilie nods.

She shows them classrooms and studios, but what Emilie sees are skinny boys with hair flopped over their faces and army jackets and sensitive hands, and she starts thinking about Philip. May is in full heat, craning her neck to take it all in. They sit in on a graphic design class Samantha's friends are in, and Emilie is next to another stocky punk rocker who does not seem to notice that she is there. May sits next to a tall boy with acne and short red hair, and in due time, she is leaning in close, letting her long hair get in his way, and Emilie wonders how someone so painfully shy can rub against boys like this. She sits closer to the punk rocker, and when he looks at her, she tries to smile at him. He whispers, "You okay?" and she nods yes. He goes back to his screen.

They decline Samantha's invitation to see the Athletic Center, so she takes them to a cafe on campus. As they wait in line, boys come up to talk to Samantha, to hug her, to get hugs from her, to invite her places, to ask why they don't see more of her. Emilie wants to slap them. Emilie and the older girl order black coffee while May sucks at a bottle of Mountain Dew. Samantha tells them she is in love with Paris, where she was an au pair for a year abroad. Emilie looks at May and rolls her eyes, mouths "let's go" when Samantha isn't looking, and she knows May is pretending not to see, pretending not to understand. Finally, Samantha shuts up and asks them if they have any questions.

"Why is everything covered in bird shit?" Emilie says, giving Samantha her best what's-so-great-about-you stare.

But Samantha doesn't catch her tone, or pretends not to, and smiles her charming cheekbone smile and says, "If you look at a map of migratory birds, we're like at the intersection of a dozen of them—geese, ducks, you name it. They all come to Moraine State Park on their way north and south. The Native Americans called the creek 'Wechachochapohka,'" she closes her eyes and pronounces the syllables, looking very pleased, "which means 'slippery rocks.'" She laughs, delighted with herself. "Pretty gross, huh?" May chuckles and Emilie snorts, despite herself.

May asks to see the dorms, still ignoring Emilie's pointed and pleading looks, and Samantha says, "Oh, that's right, you're not staying over!" She sticks out her lower lip and says, "That sucks! And we're having such a blast!" So they tramp the birdshit paths,

122

and she keys them into a big brick and cement building, and they walk through a co-ed floor, and May almost has kittens when she sees a boy in a towel; he sucks in his gut and smiles at Samantha, says "Hey, Sam," and ducks into his room.

Back in the parking lot, free of Samantha at last, Emilie thinks only of driving away from Birdshit University. May sits in the passenger seat, and as soon as the door is closed, she looks straight ahead and says, "I really liked it. I think it's awesome."

Emilie backs out, shifts to drive, and says, "God, what if they're all like Samantha?" She says the girl's name with a breathy lisp.

May says, "She was nice. She wasn't mean. What's your problem?" She puts her feet up on the dash so she can hide under her long legs and scowl out the window.

"I just wasn't very impressed," Emilie says. May keeps glaring.

Emilie says, "Why are you so pissed off? It's only Slippery Rock."

"Why did we even come? Why did you even get my hopes up?"

"I didn't know your hopes were up."

"Whatever."

"We just came to see. I saw. I didn't like."

"Whatever."

"You can go without me. I might not even be able to afford to go."

May is crying now. "I don't want to stay in my parents' house around a bunch of people who think I'm a freak and a loser!" She gulps a big sob, and says, "This place is full of freaks and losers like us."

Finally, Emilie says, "I'm just in a bad mood. I'll think about it." May stops crying. They go to Burger King, and Emilie keeps her whole meal down. Both girls send in applications, and Donna takes them to dinner at Applebees to celebrate.

May meets a boy in an internet chat room who tells her he rides a motorcycle and studies computers at Carnegie Mellon University, which turn out to be a pair of flimsy lies. He is a chubby, grasping kid named Anton, and he is into Insane Clown Posse and pro wrestling. Emilie starts thinking of getting May to

Slippery Rock because the boys in this little bass-ackwards mill-town-cum-strip-mall suck so bad that a kid like Anton can get a girl like May to fuck him. She keeps quiet, even when May starts spinning fantasies about moving in with him after graduation. Emilie says, "What about college?" and May just shrugs.

Emilie is thinking about leaving this town in her dust. She is drawing and painting nonstop. She finishes a complicated sketch of light coming through the dirty south-facing window of the apartment, and does a series of dust motes in beams of light, including one where she covers her hands in charcoal, blacking out the margins to draw swirling motes in a flashlight beam. She plays with oil paint, but doesn't like it. She makes her mom an abstract portrait of Poughkeepsie and Magoo in acrylic, and she does a series of portraits of her parents from wedding photos she loots from her mother's closet. She buys poly-clay, and she and May make little naked people and animals with huge penises, and they giggle at the way they droop and curl when the pieces come out of the oven on a cookie sheet. May says, "Anton has a friend."

Emilie doesn't say anything.

May says, "You met him. Jeff Ruggiero. He said you're cute. He's in a band."

"What kind of band?"

"I don't know," May says, "torture metal or something like that. Anton says they're going to, like, puke jello salad on the audience and squirt fake blood like this band called Gwar."

Emilie rolls her eyes and says, "Cool."

"Whatever," May says. "You could give him a chance. You don't have to be alone."

"I'd rather be alone than date one of Anton's friends."

"What the fuck is that supposed to mean?" May says, pulling back, rearing up.

"I just . . . I just think you're better than him. He's like—"

"We're in love!" May shouts, and she is crying.

Emilie sighs. "I know, but," but she can't think of anything to say, so she just says "I'm sorry." May says she is going home, and leaves. Emilie feels like a total heel.

Emilie doesn't see much of May for the next few weeks, until she comes by on a Wednesday night. They sit in Emilie's studio, with the rolls of dirty carpet and discarded furniture, and May thumbs through the sketches, and stares into the paintings of Emilie's parents. "These are great," she says. "You've been busy."

"How are things with you," Emilie says.

"I just—" and then she is crying, and Emilie puts her arms around her friend until she gets the story: May and Anton went to the dry cleaner where he works after hours, for bondage sex. May says she was excited, into it even, when he tied her to one of the big metal racks and went down on her. She says it was great, and then he started to hurt her, and she didn't like it. He put binder clips on her breasts, on her nipples, and he whipped her with a piece of rope, and she begged and cried for him to stop, and she says she is still bruised, that it still hurts, and that he won't listen to her when she says that he should have stopped when she said stop.

Emilie spits his name: "Anton. That little fuckhead is going to pay."

May says, "I mean, I guess it's not so bad."

Emilie says, "It's like—it's like rape, May. He's at least abusing you."

"It's not 'rape' for god's sakes," May says, her voice getting high. "I mean, I said yes. It was, like, hot. I was into it. I'm not abused."

"Except for the part where you said 'no' and weren't into it."

May says, "He says he'll be nicer next time. Don't get like all Oprah on me." She says, "Don't do that jealous shit, Emilie," with a nasty sound in her voice, and leaves as Emilie sputters her protests.

Emilie thinks about calling May's parents, but she doesn't. It bothers her all week. But May is already avoiding her, and she thinks that if she tells May's parents, May will never forgive her.

Another week passes, and May comes over. Emilie can tell something is up, and says, "What happened now?"

May says, "Anton wanted me to do him in the booty."

Emilie laughs. "Like, with what?"

"He wanted to be screwed with a strap-on, so we went to the porno store out by the airport, but Anton is cheap and it was like a $140, so we went to a hardware store and he bought one of those little toilet plungers and some Vaseline."

Emilie says, "What the fuck? Really?"

May says that they went to a park in the rain, and he dropped his pants and got down on all fours, and she stuck the plunger handle through the fly of her jeans and gave him what he wanted.

Emilie giggles until she starts to snort like Magoo, who has something wrong with his sinuses.

May smiles too. "So, he's into it for a while, and it's kind of gross, but whatever, and then he's screaming and shouting and kicking at me, and then he's rolling around on the ground crying and holding his ass, and he's telling me I hurt him, and I'm like, whatever, pervert."

Emilie says, "What did you do?"

"We went back to our cars and I stuck the plunger to his windshield and told him to fuck off. I think we broke up. I don't want to ever see him again."

Emilie guffaws.

"Do have your stuff from Slippery Rock?"

"Yeah."

"Can we talk about that some more?"

The girls get letters from Slippery Rock on the same Thursday afternoon. First Emilie goes to May's house, where May's mom bakes box-mix cupcakes and kisses them both on the cheeks and cries and tells them they are becoming women. It is the same thing she said to them when they got their periods, and the girls enjoy the attention while they roll their eyes at May's mom behind her back. When the cupcakes are done and they have eaten their fill, they go back to Emilie's house to tell Donna because they know she will let them drink to celebrate.

As Donna pours them tumblers of Fat Dago, they call admissions from Emilie's phone, and they both accept. The woman from admissions tells Emilie's ma that she will probably qualify for work study and other need-based aid, and as it starts to feel real, Emilie gets excited about going away to college. Emilie is dreaming of long artistic fingers and boys with floppy hair. But she is also excited about painting classes with real models; she is beginning to feel the pull of a life outside of her mother's red-wine, dog-piss existence, and it is thrilling.

May's shit-brown Ford Fiesta that smells like antifreeze finally dies, and her dad gets her a shit-brown Ford Escort that smells like mildew. Her dad says the white smoke from under the hood is nothing to worry about. She asks Emilie to go apply for jobs with her. Emilie agrees to drive her around in her mom's car to put in applications.

They drive out to the new airport, where retail jobs pay as much as two dollars more per hour, and Emilie circles it for half an hour to save parking money while May goes inside. "The lady at Au Bon Pain told me that they don't even hire kids for fast food jobs. There are too many unemployed old people," she says.

May puts in applications at Barnes and Noble and Old Country Buffet, Super Steak and Shake, and Macy's. She applies at a video game store, at Ikea, and at Regal Cinema. She goes armed with a stack of computer-printed resumes. She draws the line at Walmart. At every stop, she asks if Emilie wants to apply to any of the stores with her, but Emilie turns her down flat. When they pull up to the craft and hobby store that sells art supplies, she looks at Emilie and says, "You're going to apply here, right?"

Emilie says, "I don't really feel good," and May gives her a dark look and slams the car door. She comes back in fifteen minutes and doesn't talk to Emilie during the drive home. Emilie is glad; she doesn't want a job, doesn't need a job.

May gets hired at Manny's Texaco convenience store at the bottom of Emilie's hill.

When they finally graduate from high school, May's parents throw her a party. The girls are surprised to find that they can make a list of twenty-two other kids who they don't hate, and May doesn't mind when Emilie makes it her party, too, though May tells Emilie not to say anything because her mom is being weird about it being May's party, not Emilie's. May says her mom thinks Emilie's mom should pay for her own party. May's mom listens to Rush Limbaugh on the radio when she is at work, and tries to get May to talk about politics.

The girls make long paper chains and fill balloons from a

rented tank of helium. They bake, sneaking puffs of May's mom's cigarettes, and they go to the Giant Eagle for bite-sized candy bars, ice cream, soda, and chips. They decorate the front porch with a plastic banner that says "Welcome Home" on one side and "Congratulations!" on the other.

May puts on a new tight-fitting strapless dress with a slit skirt, and her dad comes up from the basement long enough to pout and fume and tell her she looks like a slut, but her mom makes him go back downstairs and leave the girls alone. Emilie wears a green taffeta dress her mother bought her to be a bridesmaid for her Aunt Minnie's wedding. She likes the emerald color, but she feels weird as people arrive and she is the only one dressed up like a tissue paper flower. The dress also pinches her under her arms, and she begins to worry that she is gaining weight and stays away from the snacks as much as she can stand to.

Kids come up on the concrete slab porch and ring the doorbell. Will Negrete comes, with his olive skin and soft curls and kissable lips, and his beautiful blond pixie girlfriend from Sewickley, and Emilie is jealous.

Ann Henry comes, with her older, geeky, adopted Korean cousin Leo; Ann's family is super religious and won't let her go out without a chaperon. Emilie can sense May's energy, her yearning—May is obsessed with Asian guys.

Ann Henry is only a rising junior, but she is very mature, and she tells Emilie that her mother found porn on the family computer, and her parents tried to blame her brother, but he proved to their mom that it was her father's porn, and she and her mom are praying for guidance and forgiveness. Emilie pats her hand, happy that Ann feels like she can tell her all of these juicy tidbits.

They follow thumping music downstairs to the rec room in time to see Don Schaefer ask May to dance. Don is tall, with sandy hair and pale skin, and he constantly hits on band girls, but never really gets anywhere with them.

"To 'The Thong Song'?" she asks him, her eyes darting around the crowded room.

"Why not," he says, and tries to grind against her.

"Get off me!" she says, pushing him away and running upstairs.

Emilie follows, and May tells her that she and Don hooked up in the band room before the end of school, and that he thinks they are going out. Emilie asks her what she means by "hooked up" and gets May to admit she let him finger her and that she got him off through his jeans. "But he didn't know what he was doing, and he had bad breath," she says.

May dries her eyes and they go back downstairs. May's parents have a nice house, but May gets too nervous to talk with more than one person in the room, so Emilie plays hostess. Emilie doesn't notice when May disappears with Leo, but Don Schaefer does, and when they come back an hour later, he tries to start a fight with Leo.

He pushes Leo, and Leo is sweating and shaking and saying, "Please, you misunderstand, I did nothing," over and over. Will Negrete pulls Don back into the crowd gently, and Emilie sighs and thinks, Now there's a man.

Leo makes Ann leave, but Don Schaefer is now threatening to kill himself, and May is burning red with embarrassment. Emilie pulls her aside and May tells her that they made out, and it was okay, and then she tried to give Leo a blowjob, but he freaked out because she is underage. "He had such smooth skin," she says. "I'm so, like, pissed off. I wish everyone would just go home."

Don Schaefer runs out of the house, chased by half the guests, and flings himself into Oakdale Creek. Emilie tells May she should go say something to him, but May has reached the limits of embarrassment and is angry. Finally, she walks down the hill in her sexy strapless dress and stands on the lawn above the creek where Don Schaefer is lying prostrate in half an inch of water. She shouts at him, "I'm not your girlfriend! I never said I was!"

He hollers back, through tears, "I thought you were the one." Then he tries to stick his face into the water, but can't get his mouth and nose in at the same time.

"Get out of the creek! You're making a fool of yourself."

"I don't care!" he says, sobbing into the trickle of water running over slimed gravel.

"Kill yourself then, you idiot. I hate you!" And she is embarrassed and crying, and she stumbles as one of her heels sinks into the sod.

May goes back inside, and leaves a handful of guests to deal with Don. Emilie follows her, and takes May into the bathroom to cry it out. She tells her she wanted the party to be special. "When am I ever going to get to fuck an Asian guy again?" she sobs into Emilie's green taffeta. Emilie feels her own virginity like a gallstone.

They go to Emilie's to smoke a joint and have a few glasses of wine before bed, and May sleeps in the studio on the old rolled-up carpet.

May and Emilie wake to a terrible smell in the old apartment, and it gets worse as the morning gets hotter. Emilie finds a trash bag and starts packing up takeout boxes and the little white bags Donna's pills come in. They fill the recycle bins with empty wine bottles, and May washes all the dishes, using laundry soap because there is no dish detergent. Emilie starts to pull the old Christmas tree down the stairs, but sees the piles of dog feces fossilized to the carpet and remembers why it is there. She muscles a window open and lights a vanilla creme candle. May is still wearing her fancy dress, singing "La Vida Loca" as she winnows away at the heap of plates and glasses and pots and pans when Emilie finds the stashed envelopes with the college's seal in the upper left corner. She starts pulling them out and makes a pile six inches high on the table.

She opens them and reads them, one by one. They are requests for financial aid forms; Emilie reads the short letters asking for Donna to fill out the forms, reminding her of deadlines that are months past. She opens big envelopes with instruction sheets and return envelopes and state and federal forms printed on newsprint. One letter says, in large red letters, "The final deadline to be considered for public and private aid is May 15."

May gives up the fight when she sees Emilie sitting in the living room drinking a glass of wine. She goes back to the kitchen and gets herself a clean glass and pours herself a few fingers. She says, "I'm sweaty."

Emilie doesn't feel like talking, and May says she is going to go wash up and sleep in her own bed for a while. Emilie says she is going to hang around and wait for her ma to come home.

Donna comes through the door at eight thirty and heads right for the couch. "Look at this place!" she says. "You girls really did a number on this place!" She gets a clean wine glass from the kitchen shelf and pours herself Dago red up to the rim. "Hell of a day," she says, chugging it down and getting a refill. "I was down at Mickey's, and who should come in but Harry Bucci, your dad's old pal from high school. And we sat there and had a few cocktails," she remembers her drink and polishes it off, "and doesn't he tell me he had a crush on me the whole time I was with your dad! I can't tell you—" she looks around for the bottle, and realizes she has left it in the kitchen. She goes out to top off and comes back in with a large plastic tumbler. "What was I saying?"

"Ma, I need to talk to you."

Donna starts clucking. "Oh dear, oh dear, what's the matter, Mon Emilie?" She downs half and slides back onto the couch.

Emilie shows her the stack of correspondence, which she has sorted and organized, with the most incriminating letter, the one marked "Final Deadline," on top.

"Oh, now, don't you worry your head over that junk, kiddo," Donna says. "We'll take care of that, it's just paperwork."

"Ma, you said you were going to do this stuff. The deadline is passed. I don't even know if I can go now."

"Don't you take a tone with me," Donna slurs, and she downs the rest of the tumbler and shakes it at Emilie. Emilie fills it halfway, but Donna gestures for more with the glass and slops it all over the pile of mail. Emilie tops her off and ignores the mess.

"How am I supposed to go to school?"

"You don't care about school," Donna says. "You think you're so smart. I know! I know! You just want to get away from your old momma. You just can't wait to leave me in the dust," she says. "Goddamn bastard sons of bitches, all of you."

"No, Ma, I just want to go to school."

"You'll forget all about me, you ungrate. Ungrate."

Emilie is crying and shouts, "Fuck you! Fuck you!"

Donna hiccoughs and says, "How dare you! Get your poor ma some more wine," but she is three sheets and passing out.

Emilie sits in the living room crying. She drinks some more, but it is too much like her mother, and she is too angry and heartbroken.

She gets up, spent, and toddles down the corridor to the bathroom, thinking, despite her pain, "I am toddling." She sits on the closed lid of the toilet for a while, leaning her head against the sink, pondering her mother's betrayal. Then she uncaps a brown bottle of hydrogen peroxide and drinks a long bitter drink.

The vomiting is like nothing ever, and she regrets it, but she's in for a penny, in for a pound as her memaw would say, and she pukes in the bathtub and on the floor, where she curls up, exhausted, and goes to sleep.

She wakes to her mother's staccato: "Emilie! Emilie! Emilie! Emilie!" Donna gets her cleaned up, muttering, "My baby, oh my baby!"

When Emilie is propped up in her bed, Donna calls in sick and starts cleaning up, loading baskets with dirty laundry and emptying ashtrays into a plastic shopping bag. She sits on the edge on Emilie's bed and says, "Oh, Mon Emilie, you and me need to talk." She makes her voice go all little-girl shy and sweet, the voice she uses when someone is mad at her, the voice she uses when she wants someone to buy her a drink.

"I just—I just think this college stuff is too much. It's too much. It's going to be hard. It's going to be too hard. I think it might be too hard on you. You're—you're sickly, you're fragile, Mon Emilie. I think you need to stay home, where I can take care of you." Emilie is weak and hot-faced, and she turns towards the wall until her mother leaves, and she spends half of June and most of July in bed. May comes by and tells her about a junior volunteer firefighter with six-pack abs that she meets at the Texaco. Emilie stops thinking about Bird Shit University, and when May comes over and sits with her, Emilie doesn't have much to say, so they don't say much.

May calls Emilie from the corner store on a muggy Sunday and tells her, "I'm super bored. Come steal some cigarettes and Mountain Dew." Emilie has been watching Steve Martin in The Lonely Guy, and she thinks that she would do him in a minute, and she is bumming because she is through with high school and she has not managed to get laid.

So Emilie puts on the cleanest t-shirt she can find and sprays deodorant on it and rolls down the hill to the new neon-and-fluorescent-lit cinderblock building. Even so, by the time she gets to the bottom, she has dark circles under her arms and she can smell herself.

May is busy scratching off lottery tickets that are still connected to the pack above the cash register as Emilie slips in, grabs a bag of spicy beef jerky and an orange soda. She slinks up to the counter and says "Busted!" and May jumps.

Two big windows look out on the dry brown creek bed and the empty road, and May keeps glancing out the window as she fills a pair of plastic grocery bags with candy bars, cigarettes, and bottles of pop. Then they take turns scratching off lottery tickets, and Emilie wins five dollars. May prints them each five quick-picks for the one hundred and twelve million dollar lottery on Tuesday night.

Emilie says, "You look hot." May puts a dopey expression on her face and pirouettes in the little booth. She is wearing a short straight white denim skirt and a racer-back tank shirt that is made of some kind of tight spandex material. It is cut with a keyhole that shows May's cleavage, and she makes Emilie feel inadequate and very smelly. May is wearing contact lenses, and her hair is straight and glossy, and Emilie asks her if she's wearing a push-up bra.

She bats her eyes seductively and says, "It's a secret. Victoria's Secret." Then, "It's, like, sewn into the shirt."

May is hot—and clean—but Emilie is skinny, she reassures herself, as she takes a big bite of jerky and tries to wash it down with orange pop. The pop fills her mouth with fizz, and she ends up spitting and coughing the mouthful all over the counter and the rack of candy bars below it. May squeals "Ewwwwwwwwww!," and breaks up laughing. She gets a roll of paper towels and comes around the front of the register, and they hear the bell above the door, and a beautiful boy is leaning on the doorjamb, bent over and red faced with laughter. Emilie thinks that his hair looks like her grandpa's wavy Italian cowlick in his Air Force photo from the war. He waves his hands at them, heaving with laughter, and May is cackling, and Emilie is coughing and trying to wipe herself off at the same time. He says, "I'm sorry, I'm sorry. I shouldn't laugh," and then gasps a jubilant high-pitched "hee-hee-hee-hee." Emilie snorts, and that breaks them all up again, and May sidles up to the boy and manages to touch his arm and his shoulder. Emilie feels a sudden panic. May says, "Can I get you anything?"

"Marlborough Reds, box" he says. May goes behind the counter and stretches up to get the cigarettes from the overhead rack, her tight shirt riding up to show her flat belly, and Emilie narrows her eyes as May touches his hand and presses his change into it. He packs the cigarettes by slapping them across the heel of his palm, and he unwinds the cellophane and takes a smoke out, and Emilie has her Camel Lights out and says, "Want some company while you smoke that?" He looks at her and the corners of his mouth are crooked, and she feels his gaze like a spotlight, and to her flushed and flowering shame, she laughs a brutal, deep-bellied "Ha-yuk." He smiles his crooked stiff-lipped smile even wider, and they stand staring at each other.

He says, "My name's Jack," and extends his hand. She puts her sticky limp fish in it, and he squeezes a little too hard, and Emilie is crushed in his grip and feels herself shrinking. He smells of musky deodorant spray, and she wants to bury her face in his polo shirt. He has the dark eyebrows and soulful eyes of a movie star, and he lights her cigarette with the flick of a Zippo lighter.

May is pretty, but Emilie can talk. They smoke one after another, making a little pile of butts next to the curb, and she asks him where he went to high school. He tells her Bridgeville and says he is into video production, and she tells him she went to Oakdale, that she is an artist. May comes out and lights a cigarette and stands blank-faced and silent at the edge of the conversation. Emilie rambles and babbles, and he tells her stories about his grandpa who, before he slipped completely into senility, had over 20 sets of car keys made, so that they'd take his keys away from him and then see him hurtling by like a bat out of hell in his old Impala twenty minutes later. Emilie secretly thinks that his resemblance to her Pap, and him talking about his own grandfather, is a sign. She tells Jack that when she was little, her Pap used to try to bribe her out of crying. She tells him he'd offer her gold, jewels, furs, and rides on the QE II. If she didn't stop, she tells this boy, her Pap would sit down next to her and imitate a coyote. Jack tilts his head and freezes his mouth in a creepy way, and makes a startling sound like a baby crying. She giggles and slaps his arm and says, "Stop it! Stop it!"

Finally, when Emilie has a headache from chain smoking and smiling her clown-face grin, he asks for her phone number. She goes inside, and May doesn't say anything when she gives Emilie a chewed Bic pen and a scrap of envelope to write on. He folds it into his wallet carefully, and he waves to her from the cab of his little green pickup truck.

About the Author

A native of rural Pennsylvania, Michael Gerhard Martin holds an MFA from the University of Pittsburgh and teaches writing for Babson College and The Johns Hopkins University Center for Talented Youth. He won the 2013 James Knudsen Prize from University of New Orleans and Bayou Magazine for his story about bullying and gun violence, "Shit Weasel Is Late For Class." His fiction has been shortlisted for the Hudson Prize, The Nelligan Prize, and the Iowa Short Fiction & John Simmons Prizes, and his work has appeared in *Bayou Magazine, The Ocean State Review, Junctures,* and on Salon.com.

9 780692 294000